Donna—

CHRISTMAS IN HONEY GROVE

A BRAXTON FAMILY ROMANCE

ANNE-MARIE MEYER

For my Mom

SHE'S AN IRS AUDITOR DESPERATE TO PROVE HERSELF.

HE'S A COWBOY TRYING TO HOLD ONTO HIS RANCH.

LOVE WAS NOT ON THE AGENDA.

JENNA

"You've got to get moving or you're gonna miss your flight," Sasha said as she burst into Jenna's room and flung herself onto the already crowded bed.

Jenna had to act fast and pull her suitcase to the side to save Sasha from falling on top of it. She shot her best friend an annoyed look as she balanced the suitcase on the edge of the bed and finished shoving her underwear and shirts into it.

"I'll be fine. It's only a twenty-minute drive to the airport. And with Trent's benefits we get to bypass the TSA nonsense and walk straight into the terminal." Jenna stared at the red dress she'd bought last week.

She had originally thought it would be a good idea to wear it for her mom's traditional Christmas dinner. But now it felt like a desperate attempt to prove to her family and—even though she wouldn't admit it—to Dean that she was just fine. Somehow, showing up in a tight, low cut dress would mean her life wasn't the complete disaster it felt like.

Jenna blew out her breath as she reached across to grab the hanger she'd tossed to the side just moments ago. She was a fool to think that her family wouldn't see through her attempt. Jenna was the butt of all their relationship jokes. It didn't help that she was the only Braxton girl and that her four older brothers had just happened to find the perfect girls for themselves.

Now, instead of hiding behind their relationship failures, she was going to be the sole focus of her mother, Sondra. If she wasn't asking Jenna about her reproductive clock, she would be setting Jenna up with every single guy in Honey Grove.

Which was why showing up single in her hometown wasn't an option.

Enter Trent. Sure, they'd only been on a few dates, but she'd managed to convince him to come home with her for the holidays. Lucky for her, Trent was an easygoing guy. When she asked, he'd just laughed and said that it sounded like an adventure.

"You're packing that," Sasha said as she moved to sit up on the bed. Her eyes focused on the red dress, and a devious smile spread across her lips.

Jenna shook her head as she slipped the dress onto the hanger. "I can't. I can only imagine what my brothers would say if they saw me in this." Jenna paused to raise her eyebrows at Sasha. "I'll be the laughingstock of the family."

Sasha swung her legs off Jenna's bed and marched over to her. She grabbed the dress from Jenna, who protested but failed to get the dress back.

"You have to wear this. Dean is going to freak when he sees you in it."

And there it was. The one thing Jenna had asked her best friend not to do. Mentioning Jenna's stupid crush—and her even stupider kiss—was not cool.

That was her past, and she didn't want to think about it.

"Don't," Jenna said as she lunged forward to grab the dress away from Sasha.

"You'll regret it if you don't bring it with you. After all, you'll want to strut your stuff in front of *Dean*." Sasha wiggled her eyebrows as a ridiculous smile spread across her lips.

Heat permeated Jenna's cheeks as she glared at her best friend. "I should have never told you about that," she said as she made another attempt to get the dress away from her.

Sasha laughed as she dodged. "Come on, girl. I've never seen you react that way to a guy before. You came back with stars in your eyes." Sasha held the dress in the crook of her arm so she could thread her fingers together and bring her hands up to her cheek. She blinked a few times like an anime character.

Jenna growled and glared at Sasha. "You better watch it. I might never come back with treatment like this." She marched over to her suitcase and zipped it shut with a resolute sound.

Sasha gasped, but Jenna chose to ignore her. Just as she set her suitcase upright on the carpet, the doorbell rang. Jenna cast one last stern look in her friend's direction and then walked out into the hallway. She already knew who was on the other side of the door. Trent.

He was her semi-boyfriend and her attempt to forget Dean and everything that had happened when she went back to Honey Grove for her brother Jonathan's wedding.

Her kiss with Dean was a stupid result of stupid feelings. She shouldn't have ever allowed herself to get involved with him. He was practically a Braxton himself. He'd been raised in their house, and had ended his senior year as their foster kid. He was definitely not someone she should entertain feelings for.

Especially not with her track record of relationships.

Jenna pushed out her thoughts of Dean and opened the door. Trent was wearing a black knit jacket with a red check-ered scarf. His hands were shoved into his jacket pockets, and when his dark brown eyes landed on Jenna, he smiled.

His perfectly white and straight teeth shone back at her.

"Hey, beautiful," he said as he stepped up and brushed his lips against Jenna's cheek.

Jenna reached up and pulled him into a hug. Then she waved him in. "Come on, I'm almost done. Then we can get out of here."

Sasha came over with Jenna's suitcase in hand. "Here you go," she said setting it down next to them. Sasha then folded her arms as she leaned one shoulder against the wall and stared at them with a strange smile on her lips.

Desperate to leave before Sasha said something embarrassing, Jenna grabbed her jacket from the nearby closet and slipped on her boots. Then she shouldered her purse and leaned forward to wrap an arm around Sasha, pulling her close.

Sure, Sasha might love to make her feel uncomfortable, but Jenna loved her friend and was going to miss her. "Have a great Christmas," Jenna said as she pulled back.

Sasha grinned. "Will do." Then she glanced over at Trent. "Take care of her," she said as she narrowed her eyes and pointed a finger at him.

Trent's smile faltered as if he wasn't sure what to say. He let out an uncomfortable laugh and reached for Jenna. He tugged Jenna's arm gently. "Will do," he said, reaching down to grab the suitcase. "Are you ready?"

Jenna nodded. She buttoned up her peacoat and glanced at Sasha. "I'll see you after the new year."

Sasha saluted her and followed as Jenna and Trent walked out into the hallway. She waved one final time and then shut the door, leaving Jenna alone with Trent.

Realizing that she was officially on her way back to Honey Grove, Jenna's stomach sank. She'd spent all of her time since she got back trying to forget Dean and what had happened. Now, she was headed back to the belly of the beast.

"You okay?" Trent asked as he glanced over at her. He was carrying her suitcase as they made their way to the elevator.

Jenna laughed, but it came out strained and nervous. Embarrassment crept up inside of her as she forced down her worries and smiled. "Just headed home, you know?"

Trent reached out and pressed the down button. "Eh, it can't be that bad. It's just your family, right?"

Jenna snorted. "With my mother and brothers, it's not just *family.*" The elevator doors opened, and they both stepped in, turning to face the doors as they closed.

"Should I be nervous?" Trent asked with a mischievous glint to his eyes.

Jenna studied him. She contemplated telling him yes, he should be nervous. But she didn't want him to change his mind, so she just shrugged. "As long as you're prepared for anything, you should be fine."

The elevator came to a stop, and Jenna and Trent stepped off. They crossed the foyer of her apartment building and out the sliding doors. The cold Seattle air slammed into them, causing Jenna to raise her shoulders and burrow into the protection of her jacket collar.

Trent led the way over to the black BMW that was parked next to the sidewalk. He opened the side door and held it as Jenna slipped onto the seat, then he threw her suitcase in the trunk. Trent slipped onto the seat next to her and told the driver they were ready.

They pulled into traffic and were on their way to the airport. Trent pulled her hand over to his lap and entwined her fingers with his.

Jenna tried to allow herself to get lost in the feeling of Trent holding her hand. And in any other circumstance, butterflies would have been assaulting her stomach. But, instead, dread filled every corner of her mind.

Dread that she was headed back home. Back to her mother who wanted nothing more than to get all her kids married off as soon as possible. Back to a place where everyone else had someone that they loved and cared about. They were in long-term relationships—opposed to her two-week one.

She was headed back to the place where she'd lost herself over the summer. Where she'd allowed herself to feel something for Dean that she'd kept at bay for a very long time. That she'd convinced herself she couldn't feel.

Jenna and long-term relationships didn't mix. She couldn't hold onto anyone—just ask her very long list of ex-boyfriends.

The last thing she needed was to attempt a relationship with Dean just to break it off weeks later. Where would that put her family? She would never want her family to have to choose between them—and not just because they might choose Dean over her.

She needed to focus on Trent and the fun they were having together. She needed to forget Dean and move on, just like she was hoping he'd done with her. It was foolish of her to entertain thoughts of something more.

And even though it felt impossible to forget Dean, she was going to work hard to keep her goal at the front of her mind.

The car pulled up to the passenger drop-off zone at the airport, snapping Jenna from her thoughts. Trent shot her a smile as he pulled on the door handle.

Jenna stepped out—narrowly avoiding a speeding cab that whizzed by. Her heart pounded in her chest as she glared after the driver. Trent yelled at the cab as he walked around and rested his hand on her shoulder. "You okay?" he asked.

Jenna nodded. "Yeah. I'm just ready to get this vacation over with."

Trent chuckled as he led her over to the trunk and pulled out both of their suitcases. "Well, as a pilot, I do have flight benefits. You say the word, and we can be in Fiji for a tropical Christmas."

Jenna curled her fingers around the handle of her suitcase as she followed Trent. "Oh, my mom would freak if I left."

Trent glanced down at her. "It's that intense, huh?"

Jenna scoffed as they walked into the airport. She waited for Trent to take the lead. He was studying the signs above them and then nodded to the left.

Confident that Trent knew where he was going, Jenna quickened her pace to catch up to him.

"Just wait until you meet my mother. She seems sweet, but she's ruthless. And she's a professional meddler."

Trent chuckled as he stepped up to the TSA agent who was checking tickets. Jenna pulled up her ticket on her phone and handed it over with her ID. The agent took them, and Jenna turned her attention to Trent.

"And my brothers..." She allowed her words to linger in the air as she sucked in her breath.

"I have brothers," Trent said. He nodded at the agent, who had given back his ID and phone.

Jenna retrieved hers as well and headed toward the conveyor belt. She started to unpack her electronics and liquids. "Not like mine," she said, raising her eyebrows at Trent.

Trent was slipping his belt off and laid it in the bin next to her shoes. "Are you trying to scare me off?" He shook off his coat and folded it.

Jenna snorted. "I'm not trying to scare you off, per se. Just trying to prepare you. Preparation is key for surviving a Braxton family Christmas."

Trent nodded as he stepped up to the X-ray machine. "I'll keep that in mind."

The TSA agent waved him through, and before Jenna could follow after him, a family of six beat her to the machine. She stood there, watching Trent gather his things. He slipped on his shoes and was working on his belt when she sighed.

This was a mistake. A huge, gigantic, colossal mistake. She should be staying away from Honey Grove, not bringing an unsuspecting guy into the middle of her family drama. Add in her unknown—and, frankly, repressed—feelings for Dean, and this was going to be a Christmas from hell.

2

DEAN

Dean stared at his computer, trying to focus his thoughts. If he didn't get the order in by three, Big Savings might not be able to get the items to them by Christmas.

No food meant no Christmas dinner. And no Christmas dinner meant a shelter with very upset people.

Dean cleared his throat as he blinked at the numbers in front of him. And, just like he'd done every few seconds for the last thirty minutes, his gaze dipped down to the time.

Two forty.

Jenna should be in the air by now. On her way here—to Honey Grove.

Dean scrubbed his face as he looked up and closed his eyes. He really needed to get a grip. He had a shelter to run. People depended on him to keep his cool, to have a level head. They needed a place that ran like clockwork.

He couldn't keep thinking about the way Jenna's lips felt against his. That one little memory of her had his heart racing, and it distracted him from his duty. The one he'd taken upon himself when he located his mom, who'd disappeared when he was fifteen. She'd been on drugs and barely conscious, so he dedicated his life to helping those in need.

And when she died, Dean invested what little he had in starting the non-profit Humanitarian Hearts. This place was his whole world. He wanted to help those who had lost everyone. The people society forgot.

So he needed to stop obsessing about Jenna and focus.

A soft knock on his door drew Dean's gaze. He bounced forward on his chair and rested his fingers on the keyboard. He waited for a moment—just to make sure that he didn't seem too eager—and mumbled, "Come in."

The door handle turned and the release clicked. He waited, while keeping his gaze trained on his screen, to see who was coming in.

The door flew open, and Jackson stood there with a wide grin. He and Isabel married right before Isabel's father passed away, and then he whisked her back to New York, where they'd been living for the last few months.

"I knew you'd be in here with your nose to the grindstone," Jackson said as he stepped into Dean's office. Isabel appeared behind him. They were both wearing jackets, and their noses and cheeks were bright pink from the cold snap Honey Grove was having.

Dean laughed as he stood up, pushing back his chair, and made his way over to them. After a pounding hug from Jackson and a soft hug from Isabel, he pulled back and smiled.

"I didn't know you were getting in so early." He furrowed his brow. "Does Mama Braxton know you're here yet?"

Jackson scoffed and shook his head. "If she did, do you think she'd allow us to come here?"

"We're hoping to avoid the whole, 'when am I going to get grandbabies' conversation," Isabel said. There was a hint of pain in her voice that confused Dean.

He glanced over to Jackson, whose smile had tightened.

They locked gazes, and Jackson shook his head slightly. This seemed like a topic that Dean didn't want to touch, so he clapped his hands together. "Are you ready for tonight?" he asked.

Mama Braxton had sent out an email to the entire family laying out her plan for Christmas. She had dinners, movies, and even a Nativity play mixed with tree decorating and caroling. Every minute of every day was planned. She had wake-up times and bedtimes as well. It was a little excessive, but no less than what they expected from Sondra Braxton.

Jackson took a seat and rubbed his hands on his thighs. "Yeah, we got the email. Mom definitely went a little overboard this year. It's like, since most of her children are in relationships, she can finally have that Rockwell Christmas she's dreamed about."

Dean laughed, though Jackson's comment stung a little. He wasn't in a relationship. In fact, ever since his little episode with Jenna over the summer, he'd stayed as far away from a relationship as humanly possible. Throwing himself into his work as a distraction.

Heat rose up inside of Dean as he glanced over at his best friend. He wondered if Jackson suspected something had happened between Jenna and him. Then Dean pushed that thought from his mind. If Jackson knew, he would never hear the end of it.

There was one rule a friend of a Braxton had to follow: keep your hands off of little Jenna Braxton. Period.

Clearing his throat, Dean fiddled with the stack of paper on his desk. Isabel and Jackson were talking about a text that Isabel had just been sent.

"An SOS from Tiffany," Isabel said as she reached down and grabbed her purse. "We're being summoned. James and Layla aren't at dinner yet, so there's no Penelope to buffer." Isabel's voice drifted off at the mention of the newest little Braxton addition. She was three months old and adorable. The perfect distraction for an overzealous Sondra.

Dean studied his to-do list on his desk. Thanks to his distracted thoughts, he'd only been able to get half his work done—including the food order.

So he shrugged and clicked his tongue. "Can't help you guys. I've got some stuff to wrap up here. I'll be around later tonight." He stood along with Isabel and Jackson. He rounded his desk and shook Jackson's hand. "Give your mom my excuse?"

Jackson shot him a look. "I'll do it, but you know she won't accept. She wants the *whole* family to be there tonight for dinner and decorating. If not..." Jackson sucked his breath in slowly.

Dean nodded and followed them as they headed for his office door. "I'll keep that in mind. But with the holiday a few days away, I've got to make sure things are taken care of. And then I have to make sure everything is in place for the new year."

Jackson patted Dean's shoulder. "We'll be waiting for you," he said as he stared at Dean. And then he busted up, laughing.

Isabel shook her head. "You two. Come on, Jackson, we should get going before Tiffany's texts get more desperate." Isabel was out of Dean's office and was zipping up her coat.

Jackson chuckled as he followed his wife. Then he paused, turning to focus on Dean. "Mom will expect you to be there tonight. You have until Jenna shows up with whatever new fling she has on her arm. I'd work hard on getting done before then, or you can expect the Braxton Christmas festivities to start"— he pointed at the floor—"here."

Dean waved to them and then shut his door. As soon as he was alone, he scrubbed his face.

The mention of Jenna had him all out of sorts. Or maybe it was Jackson saying she had a "new fling." Was he right? Was Jenna going to show up with another boyfriend?

She'd told him over the summer that she hated that her relationships hadn't ever lasted longer than a Tic Tac. The one thing she craved was emotional connection—which was sorely lacking in the men she dated.

Dean leaned his back against the door and tipped his face toward the ceiling as he took a deep breath. He wasn't going to allow himself to think about whatever guy Jenna had decided to bring home to Honey Grove. He wasn't going to allow himself to remember what it felt like to pull her close and press his lips to hers. Or how it felt when she told him her fears and he trusted her with his.

He was going to ignore his desire to go back to where they'd left off this past summer. Well, before she'd ripped out his heart at Jonathan's reception—when she told him that she wanted nothing to do with him. That their kiss had been a mistake.

He wanted to forget all of that.

Groaning with frustration, Dean made his way back over to his computer. He sat down in the chair and pulled himself closer to his desk. Then he shook his mouse and leaned forward, forcing himself to focus.

Truth was, if Jenna *had* brought home a guy, he shouldn't be surprised. After all, it wasn't like he was dating her—no matter how much he wanted to.

She'd asked him to move on. Told him she didn't care about him. Told him that everything he'd felt—everything he'd told her, had been a mistake.

He was a fool to keep hoping she'd change her mind. That she would come running back to him, saying that she was wrong, that leaving had been a mistake. But she never came back.

Instead, she did exactly what she'd said she was going to do. Leave.

He needed to accept that and move on. If he didn't, then this was going to be an awful Christmas. And that's not what the

Braxton family deserved. Heck, it wasn't what he deserved either.

If Jenna had moved on, then so would he. He was going to be the most moved-on guy she'd ever met.

Determination rose up in his gut as he began filling out the food order at record speed. He wanted to finish and get over to the Braxtons' before Jenna got there. He needed to scout out the territory before she blew in with her next fling on her arm.

Even though his stomach was in knots and he was actively pushing his feelings of dread down, he would never let Jenna see what her leaving had done to him.

She was going to see that he was well adjusted and moving on. That what had happened between them had been a momentary lapse in judgement. That was all.

It was a complete lie, but he was going to have to tell it, or else he feared he'd lose his heart and his family in the process.

———

The Braxton house was completely lit up when Dean pulled up out front. Sondra had Jimmy hang lights from every ledge on the outside of the house. Tiny electric candles flickered in each of the windows upstairs and down.

There was a giant wreath on the door, and a tacky projector was shining sparkles across the whole front of the white two-story house.

Dean chuckled as he turned his car off. After slipping his keys into his jacket pocket, he grabbed the bottle of wine he'd picked up on his way over.

Just as he opened the driver's door, headlights blinded him. He paused, watching a car pull into the Braxtons' driveway and idle.

Dean didn't recognize the car. He knew every Braxton vehicle, and this Chevy Malibu didn't look familiar at all. After a few seconds, the headlights went out and the engine shut down. The passenger door opened, and a man stepped out. And then Jenna's head popped up from the other side of the car.

A sick feeling grew in the pit of Dean's stomach as he watched her laugh and round the hood of the car. The man was waiting for her. Once she caught up to him, he held out his hand, and she grabbed it while wrapping her other hand around his elbow.

Heat rose up inside of Dean as he watched them walk across the driveway and up the front steps. Jenna didn't knock; she just opened the door, and both of them disappeared inside.

Dean pulled his foot back into his car and slammed the door. He threw the wine bottle into the seat next to him and pounded his hands on the steering wheel.

Well, that was just great. All his positive self-talk went right out the window. And all it took was seeing Jenna holding onto another man's arm.

"Idiot," he scolded himself as he rubbed his face with his hand. His gaze returned to the front of the Braxtons' house. He could see Jenna through the window of the living room, laughing as she held onto the loser she'd shown up with.

Jonathan was talking to the two of them, and it didn't look like Jonathan was going to do anything. Instead, he just smiled and nodded as Jenna said something.

Then they all laughed like the picturesque family they were. And Dean was the eleventh wheel that didn't really belong.

For so long, he'd told himself he was a Braxton. That Jackson's family was his family. And for most of his life, that had been true. He had never felt like a burden on the family. Sondra and Jimmy had welcomed him with open arms.

But it didn't feel the same. Not since Jonathan's wedding.

Not since Jenna.

Feeling defeated, Dean slipped his key into the ignition and turned it, the engine roaring to life. He hated what he was doing. Hated that he was driving away from the only place he wanted to be tonight. But he couldn't stay.

He threw his car into reverse and moved to look over his shoulder just as a fist pounded on his window. Dean cursed and slammed on the brake. He pushed the gear into park and rolled his window down to see James peering into his car.

"Where you going, man?" he asked. His breath puffed out in front of him.

Dean cleared his throat as he peered behind James to see Layla clutching a car seat. Her teeth were chattering as she bent her knees, trying to generate warmth.

Dean forced a smile. "I forgot the wine," he said, shrugging and resting his elbow on the steering wheel so that James couldn't see the front seat.

James furrowed his brow. "What?"

"Your mom—"

"Nah, she doesn't care. She's waiting for all of us to get inside so she can start dinner. If you make a run to the store, you'll be making us all wait." James reached to grab the door handle. "Come on," he said as he opened the door.

Dean reached forward and turned the engine off. Then he pulled out his keys and slipped them back into his jacket pocket. James stepped to the side so that Dean could climb out of his car. Once his feet were on the ground, James moved to shut the door, effectively cutting off Dean's escape route.

Dean took a deep breath as he moved to stand next to Layla. "Hey," he said, smiling down at her.

She glanced up and smiled at him. "Merry Christmas, Dean." Then she turned to face James. "Can we go inside now?"

James nodded and held out his arm. Layla shuffled over to him, and James laid his arm on her shoulder.

He grabbed the infant car seat and glanced over at Dean. "Coming?" he asked.

Dean nodded, trying to ignore the hollow ache in his chest.

He had to drop his gaze from the perfect family standing in front of him. They seemed so happy. Happier than he'd felt in a long time. "Yep. I'm right behind you."

James smiled and then led Layla up the driveway and around the back of the house. Dean followed behind them, taking in a few deep breaths of the crisp night air. He needed a moment to pump himself up.

He could do this. He could.

After all, he knew what a Braxton Christmas was like. This wasn't his first one. He'd smile. He'd laugh. And he'd hide the fact that his heart was breaking.

It wouldn't be the first time he pretended everything was okay. And he was getting pretty dang good at it.

3

JENNA

Mom's house smelled just like Jenna remembered it did at Christmas time. Sondra always insisted on buying those cinnamon-scented pinecones and putting out bowls in every room.

The cinnamon mixed with the smell of mashed potatoes and turkey, and Jenna was instantly transported back to all the Christmases of her past as she walked into her childhood home.

She took in a deep breath and glanced over at Trent, whose eyes were wide and lips parted.

"Whoa," he breathed out.

Jenna glanced around. Her mom had decorated the entire house like a department store. Every flat surface was covered in knickknacks, and above the TV was an entire mini village, complete with a train running around on its track.

"Jenna's here!" Josh called out. He was carrying a platter of mini hot dogs wrapped in phyllo dough. He was eating one when he emerged from the kitchen, and his sheepish gaze fell on Jenna.

"I told you, no sneaking food until dinner," Sondra said as she followed after him, swatting him with a dishrag.

Josh held up his free hand and then dipped down as he took a wide step away from Sondra and slipped in front of Jenna. He spun—planting a kiss on Jenna's head—before making his way toward the table full of food along the wall in the dining room.

Two hands gripped Jenna's cheeks, snapping her attention forward. Sondra was standing in front of her with what looked like tears in her eyes.

"My life is complete. My baby girl is home," she blubbered as she pulled Jenna's face toward her and kissed each cheek.

Heat permeated Jenna's skin as she tried to slip away. "Ma," she hissed as she glanced over at Trent. He was watching them with an amused smile on his lips.

"And you must be Trent," Sondra said. She dropped her hold on Jenna and held out her hand.

"That's right," he said, shaking her hand.

Sondra ran her gaze up and down him before she glanced back at Jenna. "Well, we're just excited that you could join us for Christmas. Jenna's been talking all about you."

"Yeah, for about two weeks," Josh piped in. He must have set down the platter of food and come back to join in on the conversation.

"Josh," Jenna said, glaring at him.

"Yeah, *Josh*," Beth said as she waddled up to stand next to him. Her stomach was three times the size it had been at Jonathan's wedding.

"Beth, you're huge," Jenna said and then winced.

Beth dropped her gaze. "Hey, I was trying to protect you from this guy over here and this is how you repay me?" She scoffed.

"I'm so sorry. You look beautiful, though," Jenna said as she stepped forward and pulled her sister-in-law into a hug.

Beth laughed as she patted Jenna's back. "Alright, you're earning your forgiveness."

Jenna pulled back. "I mean it. If I look half that good when I'm pregnant, I'll be—"

"You pregnant? Come on, Jenna. Never going to happen," Jonathan said as he joined them. He was holding a red Solo cup in one hand and a pig-in-a-blanket in the other.

Sondra swatted him with the dishrag. "Hey, no food before dinner, and don't put that kind of stuff out into the atmosphere. Your sister is still young. Lots of viable eggs—"

"Ma!" A chorus of male voices called out.

Sondra laughed as she held up her hands. Before she could respond, a loud beep sounded from the kitchen. "My turkey," she called out as she pushed past Jonathan and Josh and rushed into the kitchen.

"Saved by the timer, eh, little sis?" Jonathan said as he slung one arm around her shoulder.

"Guys, this is Trent," she said, motioning toward Trent, who was standing next to her with a surprised expression on his face.

"Jonathan," her brother said as he leaned forward to shake Trent's hand, all the while keeping his arm wrapped around Jenna's shoulders.

"That's right," Jenna said as she tried to wiggle out from under Jonathan. But no amount of struggling would free her. She gave up, and Jonathan laughed.

"He's married to Tiffany, who's..." She glanced around. "Jonathan, where's Tiffany?"

Jonathan took a swig of his drink. "I dunno. Hey, Tiff?" he yelled out.

A moment later, Tiffany emerged from down the hallway with a less than pleased look on her face. "What?" she asked and then folded her arms.

Jonathan fell quiet as he studied her and then muttered something under his breath that Jenna didn't quite catch. Before she could ask what was up, he shoved his hands into the front pockets of his jeans and zeroed in on Trent.

"So, what do you do?" he asked as he narrowed his eyes.

Trent studied him and then shrugged. "I'm a pilot."

Jonathan nodded as he pushed his lips up. "Nice. I bet you get to—"

Noise from the kitchen halted their conversation. Sondra was cheering, and there was a ruckus that had everyone peering in through the opening.

James and Layla had arrived. Layla was smiling as Sondra doted over the car seat on the table. James was slipping off his shoes, and just as he pulled the left one off, the back door opened once more, revealing Dean.

Jenna dropped her gaze and blinked a few times as she attempted to gain control of her pounding heart. She knew that this would happen. She knew that Dean was going to be around. So why was her heart acting like this was a big surprise? Dean was part of her family. She knew that, and yet, she slipped out of view from the back door and headed over to stand in the corner near the food table.

Maybe if she blended in with her mother's floral drapes, no one would know she was here.

Just as she walked by the food table, she tripped, and someone from under the table yelped.

Confused, Jenna dropped down and pulled back the table-cloth. Hidden under the table, with a plate of frosted cookies, was Jordan. His eyes were wide, and his lips were covered with cookie crumbs.

"What are you doing?" Jenna asked as she slipped onto her hands and knees and crawled under the table to sit next to him. Thankfully, the white tablecloth went all the way to the floor and protected them from any wandering eyes.

Once she was situated next to him, Jenna crisscrossed her

legs and studied her nephew. He was watching her with his eyebrows raised, as if he hadn't expected her to join him.

"Can I have one?" Jenna whispered, nodding at the cookies.

Jordan studied her and pulled the cookie plate a few inches closer to him, but then he sighed and held it so she could take one.

They were perfectly iced. The detail her mom had put into them was phenomenal. The snowmen had eyes, a mouth, and a perfect carrot nose. She almost felt guilty for eating one, until she slipped the buttery cookie into her mouth.

It was a scrumptious cookie. She had to hand it to Sondra, she'd really outdone herself this year.

Jenna took her time savoring the cookie. Jordan grabbed another one and took a big bite. Crumbs collected on his dark jeans, but he didn't look bothered at all. This was exactly where Jenna needed to be. Hiding out under the table, eating cookies with her nephew.

Six-year-olds really knew how to live.

"Are you excited for Christmas?" Jenna asked as she pulled another cookie from the plate.

Jordan glared at her but then snapped out of it a few seconds later. Jenna had to chuckle to herself. She knew what he was feeling. Growing up with four older brothers meant she was constantly losing her food to them.

If she even wanted a chance at eating dessert, she had to be aggressive. Fists may have been involved once or twice. But it was more likely that Jonathan's hand would be on her forehead as she attempted to fight back, while Jackson grabbed her cake and ran off with it.

It had taught her to be scrappy, that was for sure.

Jordan sighed as he shrugged. "I want Santa to bring me a Nintendo, but Dad said Santa is bringing me a baby sister for Christmas." Jordan scrunched up his nose as he stuck out his tongue.

Jenna smiled. She could only imagine how he felt. "A baby sister isn't that bad, is it?"

Jordan raised his gaze then he leaned in. "They poop in their pants. And that's gross."

Jenna nodded. "True. But you won't have to change her. Your dad will." Jenna slipped another chunk of cookie into her mouth. "What do you think of Penelope? She's cute, right? Your baby will look like her."

Jordan looked horrified as he stared at Jenna. "Penelope screams." Right on cue, a loud wail sounded from the kitchen. Jenna laughed, and Jordan waved his hand with the same petrified expression on his face. "See?" he said.

Jenna wiped at her eyes as she nodded. "Okay, but not all babies scream. Yours could be really quiet."

Jordan grabbed another cookie. "Maybe." Then he sighed. "But I'd rather have a Nintendo."

Jenna reached out and ruffled his hair. "I'll see what I can do. Maybe I can put in a good word with the big guy."

Jordan's jaw dropped open. "You know Santa?"

Jenna shrugged as she brought her knees up to her chest and hugged them. "Let's just say I know some of Santa's helpers. I'm sure they can pass the word along."

She made a mental note to talk to Josh later on about her getting a Nintendo for Jordan. Having a new sibling changed things. Jordan was going to go from the baby of the house to the older brother, and that couldn't be easy. Jenna wanted to make sure that he had a fabulous Christmas.

"Okay," Jordan said.

Jenna's heart swelled when she saw the slight smile that emerged on Jordan's lips. It made her happy that, despite her own crappy Christmas, Jordan was going to have a good one.

They ate in silence for a few more minutes before they heard Beth call out Jordan's name. Jenna pressed her finger to her lips as Jordan stared at her with wide eyes. He slipped the plate to the side as if he were trying to hide it.

"Where did that kid go?" Beth asked. Her boots became visible in the crack between the tablecloth and the floor.

"He was around here somewhere. I got distracted talking to Trent," Jonathan said. His shoes appeared next to Beth's.

There was a scraping noise above them, like someone was moving plates around.

"Hey, Jonathan, everything okay with Tiffany?" Beth's voice was hesitant. As if she wasn't sure if she was overstepping.

Jonathan cleared his throat in an uncomfortable way. "What do you mean?"

"She just seems...upset. I was wondering if it was something I could help with."

There was a moment of silence, and Jenna felt her hearing heighten. If there was something wrong, she wanted to know as well. She liked Tiffany, and if she was struggling, Jenna wanted to help.

"There you are. Where's my son?" Josh's voice interrupted the conversation, and Jenna had to stifle a groan.

"I'm looking for him. I haven't seen him for a while. He was eyeing the cookies last I knew."

"Hmmm," Josh said. Then suddenly, the tablecloth was flung to the side, and Josh's face appeared.

Jordan screamed as his dad reached in to tickle him. "What are you doing down here?" Josh asked as he grabbed Jordan's legs and pulled. Then he stopped and stared over at Jenna. "What are *you* doing under here?"

Jenna brushed off her hands. "Hanging with my nephew," she said as she crawled out after a shrieking Jordan.

"You were under there with Jordan?" Beth asked. She had her hand pressed to her lower back and was running her gaze up and down Jenna.

Jenna nodded and moved to smooth down her dark brown hair.

"We were talking about Christmas," Jordan said as Josh flung him over his shoulder.

"I don't think that was the only thing they were doing," Josh said as he turned so that Jordan's face was in view. His icing-covered lips gave him away.

"Jordan, what did I tell you about the cookies? I said *after* dinner." Beth motioned toward the bathroom. She and Josh marched Jordan off, shutting the door behind them.

"You were hiding under the table?" Trent asked. Jenna yelped and turned to see that he'd joined her.

His hand slipped to her lower back as they stood there, staring after Josh's little family.

She shrugged. "I told you my family is a lot. I needed a break," she said, turning to smile at him.

"I like them," Trent said. "They're nice."

"Jackson and Isabel just pulled up," James yelled from the kitchen.

Jenna whooped and pumped her fists in the air. She was so ready to see her brother it wasn't even funny. Ever since he ran away with Isabel, he hadn't made much time for her. She missed his witty texts that always made her laugh.

"Jackson is here," she said, grinning up at Trent as she turned and barreled right into Dean.

He was leaning on the doorframe that led from the dining room into the kitchen. Jenna tripped, and before she knew what was happening, she began to fall forward.

Someone caught her and pulled her to his chest.

"You okay?" Dean asked. His voice was deep, and Jenna's entire body stiffened. Maybe it was because her hands were sprawled across his chest. Or because his touch was burning her skin as his hand wrapped around her arm, the other one pressed into her lower back.

She stared forward, not able to meet his gaze. "Yes," she whispered

"Wow. Good catch," Trent said.

Jenna didn't have to look up to know that Dean was now looking over at Trent.

"Yeah," Dean said, pulling his hands away. Her skin felt cold in the absence of his touch. "Dean," he said, extending his hand.

"Trent," Trent replied, meeting his handshake.

They stood there, shaking hands, for what felt like a tad too long. Jenna was still trying to calm herself after her interaction with Dean, so she couldn't speak or say anything to Dean about Trent.

Heat was permeating her cheeks as she swallowed.

"I thought all of Jenna's siblings had names that started with *J*," Trent said as he dropped Dean's hand. He shoved his hands into his front pockets.

Dean smiled. "Yeah, I'm an adopted Braxton." His gaze slipped over to Jenna, and she allowed herself to meet it—if only for a second.

"He lived with us for his senior year after his dad passed away. But it wasn't anything new. He'd always been around," Jenna said, finally finding the strength to speak.

Trent nodded as Dean studied her. There was a look in his eye that was making her nervous. It was one she'd seen that summer. Before they kissed. Before she ruined everything by thinking she could have feelings for Dean.

"He's like a brother to me," she added as she forced a smile and threaded her arm through Trent's, pulling herself closer to him. She needed to remind herself that she was with Trent. Trent was her boyfriend. She liked Trent.

Dean had his brow furrowed as he looked at her. Then he glanced over at Trent and offered him a smile. "Yep. Honorary Braxton slash brother, here." He sighed as he clapped his hands together and started backing up toward the kitchen. "I should see if they need my help."

Trent had turned his focus to the food table, but Jenna kept her gaze on Dean. She hated that she was hurting him. That wasn't what she wanted. But how could she tell him that without giving him false hope?

Just before Dean slipped into the kitchen, he glanced back at her. His expression was sad, and he held her gaze for a moment. He nodded slightly and disappeared.

Jenna's heart felt as if it was breaking a little bit. She was such a horrible person. She didn't deserve Dean. He was better off without her.

Wanting to get some space between her and her regrets, Jenna let go of Trent and nodded toward the drink table. "Come on. I could use some alcohol."

4

DEAN

Well, this evening was about as crappy as Dean had anticipated. He was regretting that he hadn't just kept on driving. Then he could have avoided this entire awkward and vomit-inducing situation.

Thankfully, with all the Braxtons in one house, it was crowded. As everyone filled their plates with food, it was easy for Dean to get lost in the sea of bodies.

His plan was to camp out in the kitchen. No one was going to come in here. Everyone knew if Sondra caught you in the kitchen, you were immediately recruited for dish duty.

Which, he was totally okay with. If he was in the kitchen, elbow-deep in sudsy water, he wouldn't have to watch Jenna fawn all over her newest fling.

Leaning against the counter, Dean extended his legs out in front of him. He sighed as he pushed the edge of his fork into the moist turkey meat on his plate. Whatever Mrs. Braxton had done to the turkey was heavenly. The taste, the texture. It was divine.

Dean scooped up some mashed potatoes and cranberries and then slipped it all into his mouth. He chewed, allowing the taste to calm his ragged nerves. He wasn't really one to drown his sorrow in food, but maybe he should if Mrs. Braxton was providing it.

"Should I leave you with your plate?" Jenna's teasing voice filled the air.

Dean opened his eyes as he inhaled, causing a chunk of turkey to fly to the back of his throat. He began to cough, his eyes watering. He turned and set his plate down on the counter. Then he grabbed a glass of water and downed it in one gulp.

"I'm sorry," he said, his cheeks heating. He cleared his throat and took another drink.

Jenna was just standing there with wide eyes. "I think I should be the one to apologize for almost killing you." She raised her hands. "I come in peace." The tone of her voice was strained. As if she wasn't sure how to talk to him.

Dean hated it. He didn't want her to feel uncomfortable around him. He shook his head. "It's okay. Serves me right for having a moment with my food."

Jenna laughed as she wandered over to the refrigerator. She disappeared behind the door and reappeared with a bottle of wine. "We ran out of spirits out there," she said as she slammed the door.

Dean set his glass down and nodded. "Definitely a must," he said, offering her a smile. He hoped against hope that they could move past what had happened this summer and go back to being friends. If she truly didn't care about him, and if being with Trent was what she really wanted, then he was okay with that.

Well, he could accept it and, with time, get over it.

But he didn't want his inability to accept what she'd said to influence their friendship. He missed talking to Jenna. Like, really missed talking to her.

Jenna shot him a small smile and started walking toward the doorway. "Well, I should get back. Mom's already brought up the number of eggs I have left. I'd hate to see what else she comes up with while I'm gone. I think Trent is scared enough." She shrugged as she rolled her eyes.

Desperate to show her that he was okay, that he really wanted to move on, Dean scrambled to say, "He seems really nice." He stepped forward and held out his hand. When Jenna's gaze dropped to it, he pulled it back. What was he doing?

Jenna studied him for a moment before she nodded. "He is nice."

A silence fell between them as Dean internally yelled at himself to speak. If he was over her, he should be able to carry on a normal conversation with her.

"Have you been dating long?" he asked. He was desperate to keep her here. Eventually, the awkwardness had to dissipate, right? It was like running, the more you did it, the easier it became. Or, at least, you eventually became numb to the pain.

Jenna studied him and then sighed, as if she had resigned herself to talking to him.

It didn't really boost his self-confidence, but forcing an awkward conversation was better than attempting to avoid her all Christmas.

"Two weeks. We met at a bar and hit it off." Jenna shifted the bottle to the other hand.

Dean blinked a few times. Was she serious? She'd only just met the guy, and yet she had invited him to Christmas?

There was no way this could be real. Dean felt a small flicker of satisfaction. Jenna was trying to convince herself that she didn't care for him by bringing this fling of hers to Christmas.

Jenna was completely disregarding the fact that Dean had grown up with her. He knew her tells. He knew that when she cared about a guy but couldn't have him, she would often flirt with another guy. As if having a man in her life was the solution to all her problems.

"What?" Jenna asked, her voice taking on a sharp tone.

Dean shrugged as he grabbed his plate. He picked up his fork and resumed eating. "Nothing. I didn't say anything."

Jenna narrowed her eyes as she stared at him. "But you want to. I can see it in your eyes." She twirled her finger in front of his face. "You have the same look my brothers get when I tell them that I'm dating someone new." She clicked her tongue as she tapped her chin. "What's the word? Let me think...judgmental. That's what it's called."

She dropped her hand to her side but continued to stare at him.

Dean wasn't sure how to respond to that. He wanted to tell her that he was happy for her. That if being with Trent the pilot was what she wanted, then he would be the first to support her. But this was ridiculous. She'd only just met the guy.

"I just want you to be careful," he said as he scooped up some mashed potatoes.

This wasn't the conversation he'd pictured having with her. But at least they were talking instead of staring blankly at each other. That had to count for something.

Jenna sighed. "I am careful," she said.

Dean chewed a piece of turkey. "Then I'm happy," he said, shooting her an exaggerated smile.

He shrugged and picked up the empty glass beside him. He tipped it toward Jenna and then nodded at the bottle in her hand. "Mind if I have some?"

Jenna stared at him for a moment, as if she were trying to process what he'd just said. Then she nodded, pulling the cork from the wine bottle. "Yeah, sure."

Just as she began to pour, Sondra appeared.

Her cheeks were rosy, and even though she looked exhausted, Dean hadn't seen her this happy in a long time. "I'm so glad the two of you are here." Sondra furrowed her brow. "I'm afraid I have some bad news."

Dean straightened as he turned to give Sondra his full attention. "What's up?" If it gave him an excuse to leave, he was going to take it. Too many conflicting emotions were racing through him.

Sondra sighed and tucked some of her graying hair back into the bun at the top of her head. "There's no heat in the apartment above the garage," she said as she walked over to the kitchen sink and grabbed the dishrag that was draped over the faucet.

"That's fine, Mom. Trent and I can grab a room at the hotel in town."

Dean's ears perked at Jenna's suggestion. *A room? As in single?*

"You guys can stay with me." The words burst from him before he could stop himself.

Sondra breathed a sigh of relief. "I'm so happy to hear that. That's exactly why I was on my way here to talk to you." Sondra turned to Jenna. "You know our family rules. No sleeping in the same room if you're not married."

Jenna parted her lips to protest, but Sondra raised her finger.

"No if, ands, or buts about it, Jenna. You're staying with Dean. Jackson and Isabel are staying here, if that was going to be your next suggestion." Sondra smiled over at Dean. "Besides, Dean will be lonely. I'm sure you and Trent can help liven up his house." Sondra narrowed her eyes as she wrapped her arm around Dean's waist.

"Why don't you bring that one girl you were seeing? What was her name—Naomi?" Sondra smiled up at him.

Dean swallowed as he allowed his gaze to slip over to Jenna for a moment. A feeling of satisfaction coursed through him when he saw her deer-in-headlights look. Good. That felt like a win for him.

Sure, Naomi was cute, albeit oblivious. She'd asked him on a few dates, and he'd obliged. After all, it wasn't like Jenna was running to his arms anytime soon. But, unlike the woman who had taken his heart and stomped on it, he wasn't the kind of guy who just dated to not be alone.

If he was with someone, it was because he wanted to be with them.

"Oh, I'm not talking marriage...yet," Sondra said and then chuckled. "It would just be nice to see you happy with someone. All my other children have found their ever afters—"

"Ma," Jenna said, but Sondra just waved her off.

"I'd like to see you do the same."

Dean chuckled, even though he felt completely uncomfortable with this conversation. But he knew Sondra meant well, so he squeezed her shoulders and nodded. "I'll see what she's up to. Maybe I'll invite her to cookie making or something."

Sondra patted his chest with her hand. "You do that. It would be fun to have her join us."

Then she sighed. "Well, I better get back. If I'm not watching your father, he's going to eat all of the bacon-wrapped shrimp. And his cholesterol..." She shot her finger up into the air while making a rocket sound.

Dean nodded and returned to his plate. He could see Jenna still standing there, staring at him. Sondra made her way out to the dining room only to pause and lean back into the kitchen.

"Oh, and I forgot. As punishment for not being social, you two are on dish duty." She disappeared before either of them could reply.

Jenna turned to yell something at Sondra, but she must have seen that her mom was gone, because her shoulders dropped. When she turned back to Dean, her lips were pinched.

Dean shrugged as he shoveled food into his mouth. He didn't want to stand in the kitchen next to Jenna either. He had been looking forward to some peace and quiet.

"I'm going to go get my food and tell Trent where I am," she said softly as she grabbed the wine bottle with both hands and walked, dazed, from the kitchen.

Dean nodded but doubted that she saw him. Once she was gone, he took a deep breath and scraped the remnants of his meal into the garbage. He wasn't hungry anymore.

This was not what he wanted at all. Doing dishes with Jenna or having her and Trent over to sleep at his house. He valued his privacy, and having a couple at his house would kill any kind of alone time that he could get. But he feared Sondra more. Plus, at least he'd be able to keep an eye on the two of them.

Maybe by the end of the holidays, he and Jenna could figure out a way through the cloudy tunnel that was now their relationship. Close proximity would help. No longer could they run to their respective hideouts. They would have to face their new normal. And to be honest, that sounded like the best Christmas present he could think of.

Moving past what he felt and how hard he fell for her was exactly what he needed.

Starting today, he was going to forget Jenna.

5

JENNA

Jenna weaved through her family in search of Trent. He had to be here somewhere. She finally broke through the crowd and found him standing next to the tree, laughing with Josh. They were each holding Christmas ornaments.

Regret for leaving Trent alone washed over her. She should have known better than to leave him unattended.

Blast Dean and his ability to suck her into a conversation. She forgot all sense of time and place when he was around. She needed to keep that in mind next time she aimlessly wandered around her parents' house. She should have known he would be hiding out in the kitchen. That was his normal spot. Now she was not only going to have to do dishes with him for the next hour, but stay at his house with Trent.

Jenna forced a smile and walked over to her boyfriend. "What's going on over here?" she asked as she peeked at the ornament Trent was holding.

It was one of those tacky ornaments with two snowmen on it. In the middle was a banner that read, *Jenna and Josh '14*. Heat permeated her cheeks as she reached forward to grab it from Trent.

"This isn't the first one we pulled out," Trent said as he nudged her with his elbow. Jenna turned to see the tree was littered with every ornament her mother had insisted on getting each year. Each year she'd brought a different boyfriend home with her.

"Mom," she whispered. She couldn't find the strength to speak louder.

Sondra shrugged as she continued hanging a bird ornament. "What, sweetie?" she asked.

"Why do you still have these?" Jenna asked as she pulled down a yellowed version of the previous one. Except this one had *Jenna and Paul '10* on it.

Sondra glanced over at her. "Honey, these are your past. What do you expect?"

Jenna groaned as she pulled off another one. As her ornaments piled up over the years, it became a long-standing joke in the family. Eventually, her brothers had started getting her ones that said *Jenna and Thor '47*.

They all thought it was hilarious, but to her it was the opposite of funny. It was humiliating. Jenna cared about each and every guy she'd brought home. She always wanted her relationships to work out. Being the butt of her brothers' jokes felt like a knife had been stuck in her gut more times than she could count.

But she couldn't cry. Up until last year, none of her brothers were very in tune with their feminine side. Sure, being married had helped straighten them out, but it didn't change the fact that they saw her as the girl who couldn't hold onto a relationship to save her life.

It hurt.

But Jenna couldn't say that. Not when everyone else was

laughing. She had to smile and go along with it. After all, if she didn't want to open an ornament on Christmas day that said *Jenna and Mr. Sensitive '19* then she needed to smile and laugh it off. And act like nothing was wrong.

So she handed the ornament back to Trent, told him that she would be in the kitchen doing the dishes, and left him laughing with her brothers.

She took a few deep breaths as she walked into the kitchen. Dean was standing in front of the sink with his hands plunged into the water. Apparently, James had been recruited to gather the dishes, and a huge stack was now sitting on the counter next to Dean.

He must not have heard her come in. When she grabbed the dish towel that was hanging on the bar of the oven and stepped up next to Dean, he jumped, flinging suds everywhere.

"Geez, Jenna. You scared me," he said as he brought his wrist up to his face to wipe off the bubbles that had landed there.

Jenna winced and shrugged. "Sorry." Then her gaze dropped down to his cheek, and she leaned in. "Mind if I…?" She didn't wait for him to respond. She reached up and wiped the suds away with the towel.

Dean grew still as his gaze trailed its way from her lips to her eyes.

Her heart began to pound as she quickly dropped her hand and turned to the sink. "Sorry," she whispered. Then she flipped on the water and began to rinse the sudsy dishes that had piled up on her side of the sink.

Dean cleared his throat and shook his head as he returned to washing dishes. "It's okay. I'm glad you helped me out," he said.

It may have been the ringing in her ears, but Jenna swore that Dean's voice had dropped a bit. As if he were having a similar reaction to hers.

Stupid, stupid body.

They stood next to each other as they worked on the dishes. Jenna didn't really know what to say to Dean, and it seemed he felt the same. What surprised her most was the fact that it was okay, working in silence with him.

The occasional burst of laughter carried through from the living room, and they both would turn to glance toward the noise before returning to the sink.

"They sound like they are having fun," Dean said as he slipped a casserole dish into the soapy water. He rested his hands on the edge of the sink as if he were giving the dish some time to soak.

Jenna scoffed as she focused on rinsing the strainer, which was proving difficult. "Yeah, they would be."

Jenna felt Dean's gaze on her.

"What does that mean?" he asked as he reached over and took the strainer from her. Then he put his hand under the faucet, letting the water run off in a wide stream onto the strainer. That seemed to allow the water to actually rinse all the little holes.

Jenna sighed as she dried her hands and rested them on the counter next to her. She dipped her head down and pushed her lips back. That helped her relieve the stress in her mind and body.

"They're decorating the tree," she said flatly as she straightened and looked over at Dean.

He quirked an eyebrow as he handed the strainer over. And then realization passed over his face as he nodded. "Ah, the infamous Jenna ornaments."

Jenna swatted him with the towel. Dean tried to block her but only succeeded in flinging suds everywhere. He grabbed the dish rag and began to wipe it up.

"It's humiliating," she said.

Dean shrugged. "Then maybe you shouldn't be bringing

every Tom, Dick, and Harry home with you for Christmas," he said softly as he glanced over at her.

Jenna sighed. "Don't say that to my brothers. The last thing I need is an ornament with the names Tom, Dick, and Harry on it."

Dean's lips tipped up into a smile, and a chuckle escaped his lips. He nodded as he washed the gravy boat. "Yeah, I could see them jumping on that one."

The room fell silent as they both focused on their respective jobs. Then Jenna found herself wanting to talk, to explain to Dean that she wasn't just a girl who couldn't make up her mind. She didn't just fall for every guy she met.

"It was never my intention..." she started, but she found it hard to finish that sentence.

Dean glanced over at her. "What?" he asked.

Jenna took in a deep breath as she fiddled with the hem of the towel. She then turned to face him, smiling although it felt strained.

This wasn't what she wanted. But putting her guard down with Dean had gotten her in trouble in the past. If she wanted to keep this platonic, then she couldn't be confessing her fears and feelings to him.

She needed to keep Dean at arm's length. The last thing she wanted was to wind up Christmas morning with her name embossed next to Dean's. Her family would think it was the best joke ever—even if she wasn't laughing.

She needed to focus on keeping her distance and not falling down the well that was her feelings for Dean.

Jenna shrugged as she grabbed a plate from the stack and wiped it off. "Never mind." She peeked over at Dean to see if he had bought her lie.

He studied her for a moment before he blew out his breath and turned his focus back to the dishes. He finished washing the last few, and as he wiped down the counters, Jenna dried the remaining dishes.

Once the dishrag was hanging on the faucet and Jenna's wet towel was tucked back onto the handle of the oven, Jenna turned to Dean.

"Well, I guess we're done," she said, offering him a soft smile.

Dean nodded and then glanced over at the living room. "I guess we should go in, then."

Jenna nodded and waited for him to lead the way. After a few seconds, he clapped his hands and made his way through the doorway into the living room.

Jenna followed him and located Trent. He was sitting at the far end of the couch. He saw Jenna and waved her over.

Jenna smiled and stepped around her family members who were sitting on the floor. They were all facing the tree as Sondra stood at the outlet with the plug for the string lights in her hand. She was saying something, but Jenna wasn't really paying attention.

Instead, she was trying to ignore Dean's gaze as she sat on the armrest and balanced herself by pressing onto Trent's shoulder with her hand. She shifted until she could no longer see him.

He was confusing her. It was hard, trying to stay platonic toward him and still be in his presence. As much as she didn't want to admit it, she could see he had questions for her. And it drew her in.

But that was something she couldn't allow. Playing with fire had already gotten her burned. A relationship with Dean was off the table no matter how she sliced it. The ornaments on the tree proved that Jenna Braxton couldn't hold onto a relationship to save her life. Either she would leave, or Dean would. And Jenna wasn't sure which would be worse.

Her love life was a mess, and there was no way she was

going to drag Jackson's best friend and her parents' pseudo son into it.

Her relationships came and went, but what Dean had with the Braxtons was important. He deserved to love someone without the risk of losing his family. Even though Jenna was pretty sure that they would pick Dean over her every time, she didn't want to put them in that situation.

Besides, she could already hear her brothers asking her what she was thinking, why she would involve herself with Dean when she knew she sucked at relationships.

They would hate her. She just knew it. And she didn't want to be Jenna, the family screwup. No matter how hard it was to hear her mom ask Dean to bring Naomi around, she was going to be happy for him.

After all, she was leaving a few days after Christmas, and she had no intention of coming back until she was good and engaged. If she had to go one more Christmas watching her brothers have perfectly healthy and happy relationships with the women in their life, she was going to die. Right here, on the floor.

"Hey, everything okay?" Trent asked as he leaned forward. He kept his gaze turned to her mom to make it look like he was still listening, but his focus was on her.

Jenna rubbed her arm and nodded. "Yeah, why?"

Trent glanced over at her with his brows furrowed. "You just kind of left earlier."

Jenna felt guilty. Here she was worried about how she felt about Dean when she had a perfectly acceptable guy who'd chosen to fly across the country with her to brave her family. She was being selfish, and she hated that.

She nodded and reached out to entwine her fingers with his. "Yes, I'm fine. I can just get a tad sensitive about those ornaments," she said.

Trent wrapped his arm around her hips and pulled her

closer to him. He nodded as he rested his head on her arm. "I get it. But I'm here now, right?"

Jenna nodded. "Yep, you are." She sighed as she gave her full attention to her mother. Sondra swept her arms dramatically before she bent over and plugged the lights in.

The tree lit up as the lights began to twinkle. Everyone oohed and aahed at the way the ornaments shimmered.

Eventually, people grew tired and began packing up to go home, much to Sondra's dismay. And Jordan was feeling sick— no doubt from all the cookies he ate.

Beth was complaining that her ankles were so big she doubted she could slip her shoes on. Josh was behind her, carrying an armful of Tupperware that Sondra had set him up with.

Jonathan and Tiffany were standing by each other, but not really talking. They were busy slipping on their coats and nodding to Sondra, who was informing them what she'd put in their plastic bags.

Jenna yawned as she glanced over at Trent. He was on his phone, typing something she couldn't really read. She figured he'd tell her later. She slipped off the arm of the couch, her butt half numb, and wandered over to the door to slip her jacket on.

James rested his arm on her shoulder. "Good to have you home, little sis," he said as he leaned over and kissed her on the head.

Jenna laughed and patted his back. James had always held a soft spot in her heart. He was the gruffest of the Braxton boys, but inside, he was the sweetest. Which was why him having a daughter just killed her. He was going to be the best daddy ever to that little girl.

"That's right. It's been too long since you've come home," their dad, Jimmy, said as he pushed past James and enveloped Jenna in a hug. Her dad pressed his lips to the top of her head then pulled back, still holding onto her shoulders.

"Don't forget, doughnuts and coffee one of these mornings," he said in his big, booming voice. He gave her a wink.

Jenna nodded. "Of course, Dad. It's tradition."

Jimmy squeezed her shoulders and then dropped his hands. "Just keep it quiet when you're around your mom. I don't want to hear another word about my blood sugar. That woman has me eating kale." He scrunched up his nose.

Jenna mimicked him as she nodded and pressed her forefinger to her lips. Just then, Sondra came bustling in. She was carrying Penelope's car seat and was followed by Layla, who look exasperated.

"I know, I know, but the manual said that the base should be set at thirty to forty degrees. When I looked in there earlier, I didn't see that. I really think we should go out and check." Sondra was slipping on her shoes and had her hand poised on the door handle.

"I know, Mom, but I promise you that James measured. It's within that range. She's as safe as any baby could be."

James smiled as he took the car seat from Sondra. "Ma, there's no way I'm going to play with the safety of my daughter. Trust me, if I could pad the entire car, I would." He then shoved his thumb in Layla's direction. "Even Speedy Magee here complains I drive too slow."

Sondra parted her lips as she turned to stare at Layla, who was moving to adjust Penelope so that she could be easily slipped into her car seat.

She widened her eyes when she noticed everyone staring at her. "What?" she asked. And then she sighed, blowing her brown hair from her face. "It's more dangerous to not follow the flow of traffic," she said as she placed Penelope into her seat and began to buckle her in.

Jenna watched James and Sondra's gazes meet, and they both shook their heads. When Layla straightened, they stepped back as if nothing had happened.

"Woman, leave those two alone. They know what they are doing," Jimmy boomed as he stared Sondra down.

Mrs. Braxton shot him a look, and Jimmy humphed and proclaimed that he was going to watch ESPN. As he headed into the living room, he passed by Trent, who was wandering toward them with a confused expression.

"I was wondering where you went," he said as he draped his arm over Jenna's shoulders.

"Just saying goodbye to my brothers," she said as she stepped out of the way so James and Layla could slip out.

Sondra declared that she was going to get the room ready for Jackson and Isabel and disappeared upstairs.

"Ready to go?" he asked.

Jenna nodded and then paused, hoping he'd be okay with what she was about to tell him. "Apparently, there's no heat in the garage apartment. So we're staying with Dean." She forced a smile as she looked up at him.

Trent didn't look fazed. "I am beat. As long as there's a bed and a pillow, I'm good." He turned. "Right, Dean?"

Jenna's shoulders tightened as she glanced behind her to see that Dean had come up behind them. He furrowed his brow and then nodded. "Yep, I've got beds and pillows."

Trent clapped him on the back and waved to the door. "Then lead the way, my friend. We will follow."

Dean's gaze slipped over to Jenna and then back to Trent. After his shoes were on, he grabbed his jacket and kissed Sondra on the cheek. She'd come down the stairs with her hands tucked into the corners of a fitted sheet.

"Good night," she called.

Jenna blew her mom a kiss and then stepped out onto the porch, shutting the door behind her. Trent was right. A good night's sleep was exactly what she needed to sort out her flurry of emotions.

CHRISTMAS IN HONEY GROVE

She knew the minute her head hit the pillow, she would be out.

Trying to interpret how she felt about Dean was exhausting her, and she was ready to welcome the darkness that came from closing her eyes and allowing her body to relax.

Tomorrow she would worry about Dean. Tonight, she was going to sleep.

6

DEAN

The sunlight was shining through the crack in Dean's drapes, making it impossible for him to continue sleeping. He needed to get up. He needed to get dressed and head into the shelter. There was so much to do between now and Christmas Eve that if he spent any more of his morning holed up in his room, he was going to seriously regret it.

He knew he was just avoiding the kitchen and any common room that Jenna could be in with Trent. Thankfully, they were all exhausted when they got to his house last night, so they'd collapsed into bed and fallen asleep.

Jenna was on the guest room futon, and Trent was camped on the living room couch. And with the way Dean was feeling, the last thing he wanted was to make small talk with Trent.

He was a nice enough guy, but not someone Dean was interested in getting to know. He had enough guy friends. He wasn't looking for more.

Dean groaned as he scrubbed his face then flung off his blankets. He placed his feet on the cold hardwood floor and winced. Then he stood and stumbled into his bathroom, where he flipped on the water and waited until steam had filled the room.

After his shower, he felt more awake. He dressed and grabbed his wallet and keys from his dresser as he pulled open his door. Just as he passed by the guest hallway bathroom, the door opened, and Jenna nearly ran into him.

His gaze dropped to the towel wrapped around her body. Her skin was pink from the shower, and her hair was pulled up into another towel that was twisted around her head.

Her eyes widened as she dipped forward, as if trying to cover her body. "Sorry," she muttered.

Not wanting her to feel self-conscious, Dean tilted his face toward the ceiling. "It's okay," he said, sounding a little gruffer than he wanted to.

He hated that he was acting so weak about this. He couldn't seem to move past what had happened this summer and was clinging onto something that would never happen.

"I'll go make some coffee," he said as he kept his gaze up. He sidestepped Jenna and, once he was sure she was behind him, zeroed in on the kitchen.

He pulled out the coffee and got the machine warming up. Then he made his way over to the fridge, grabbed the carton of eggs, and set them next to the stove.

It felt strange, getting ready to cook for someone. He'd spent so much of his life single and alone. He was trying to ignore the anticipation of sitting down at the table with Jenna.

She wasn't his. He needed to remember that. If he didn't, he feared the trouble he would get himself into. The last thing he needed was to confess his feelings for Jenna.

If he wanted a breath of a chance to keep Jenna in his life, he needed to put his foolish thoughts for her behind him. What happened over the summer was over. He just needed to get his heart and mind on board, and then he would be okay.

"I'll be fine," he muttered to himself as he cracked an egg on the edge of the pan and pulled the shell apart. The egg sizzled on the hot pan. Dean leaned forward and adjusted the temperature and then continued to crack the eggs.

"Talking to yourself?" Jenna's voice snapped him from his thoughts.

Dean jumped and, in the process, managed to slide his hand against the hot pan. Searing pain shot through his fingers as he brought them up to his lips.

Jenna's eyes were wide as she stared at him. Her cheeks hinted pink as she rushed over to the sink and turned on the faucet.

"Come here," she said, waving him over.

Dean nodded and walked over. Jenna wrapped her fingers around his wrist and shoved his hand under the cold water.

"You were always easy to startle," she said, glancing over at him.

Dean was trying to calm his pounding heart, and he took note of how close Jenna was. She was only inches away, staring up at him.

He'd never noticed until now how tiny she was. The top of her head barely made it to the top of his shoulder. And yet, she had a personality as strong as her mom. Big and commanding, yet loving and kind.

She was the kind of person that could be best friends with anyone. Dean felt his breathing go heavy as he studied her.

Jenna held his gaze for a moment before she uncurled her fingers from his wrist and stepped back. She cleared her throat and adjusted the cream-colored sweater she had on.

"Sorry," she whispered as she dragged her fingers through her now dry hair. "I didn't mean to startle you."

Dean wiggled his fingers under the water and shrugged. Then he pulled his hand back and shook off the excess water. He reached over and grabbed a paper towel from the roll. It took a few tugs to pull a sheet off.

Then he wrapped the towel around his fingers and turned to smile at Jenna. He wanted her to think that he hadn't read into what had happened—even though he had.

"It's okay," he said as he winked at her. He instantly regretted it. What was he doing? What was wrong with him?

Jenna pinched her lips together as she stared at him. The coffee maker chimed, and she nodded. "I'll get the coffee while you finish the eggs?" she offered.

Dean nodded, thankful that she was no longer staring at him. He welcomed a job. It allowed him to forget the thoughts that were rolling around in his mind.

Once the eggs were plated and the toast was buttered, Dean turned around to find Jenna sitting at the table. Her hair was tucked behind her ear, and she was reading from yesterday's newspaper, which he had set off to the side.

He took in a deep breath as he allowed himself to stare at her for only a moment before clearing his throat and walking over to deposit her plate in front of her. Then he set his down on the other side of the table.

He went back for Trent's plate and set it next to Jenna. "Where's Trent?" he asked, hating the way the guy's name felt on his tongue.

Jenna paused with her fork halfway to her mouth. Then her eyes widened as she stared toward the living room. She almost looked like she'd completely forgotten that Trent was there.

"Trent," she called as she set down her fork and stood. Then she disappeared into the living room.

Dean stared down at his eggs. What was he doing? Why did he have to bring up her boyfriend? Now he would be joining them for breakfast. Dean's chance for some one-on-one time with Jenna was now out the window.

Great.

Jenna came back into the kitchen. She was rubbing her neck

as if she were stiff. Dean furrowed his brow and made a mental note to ask her about that later.

"Everything okay?" he asked as he took a bite of eggs, hoping he looked nonchalant.

Jenna glanced over at him and nodded as she sat on her chair. "He's taking a shower and will join us shortly."

Dean stifled a wince as he nodded and began shoveling food into his mouth. He was hoping to finish his breakfast and leave before Trent got to the kitchen. There was no way he wanted to stand by and watch as Jenna and Trent laughed and joked together.

He wasn't that cruel to himself.

"Wow. You're hungry," Jenna said as she took a bite of her toast.

"I'm late for the shelter," he said as he stood and walked over to the sink, setting his plate next to it. Then he grabbed the two slices of toast and held them in his mouth. He filled his coffee cup and pushed the lid on—all while taking bites of his toast.

Just as he made his way over to the door to grab his jacket and shoes, Trent came wandering into the kitchen with damp hair and an annoyingly nice smile.

"Good morning," he said, nodding in their direction. Then he furrowed his brow as he stared at Dean. "Heading out already?"

Dean nodded as he shoved his foot into his shoe. "Yep. I'm late actually."

Trent poured a cup of coffee and took a drink as he moved his gaze from Jenna to Dean. "What's on the schedule today?" he asked.

Jenna pointed to the plate of eggs and toast next to her. "Dean made you breakfast," she said.

Trent nodded and moved to sit next to her. Then he turned to focus on Jenna. There was something in his gaze. Something

CHRISTMAS IN HONEY GROVE

that caused Dean to stop moving. He pulled his jacket on slowly as he waited to hear what Trent had to say.

"I've got some bummer news," Trent said as he studied Jenna.

"Yeah?" Jenna pushed her eggs around on her plate.

"George called and asked me to cover the Paris flight on Christmas." He winced as he studied Jenna. "I know I said I'd spend it with you, but his ex-wife agreed to let him have his kids. I have to help the guy out." He leaned forward and wrapped his fingers around Jenna's hand.

She looked at him and let out her breath slowly. "You're his only option?" she asked.

Trent nodded. "Everyone else has a family. I'm the only... single guy," Trent said slowly.

Dean watched Jenna as she took an exaggerated breath and nodded. "It's okay. It's sweet of you to think of George." She smiled.

Trent began to lean forward, and Dean took that as his cue. "Lock up when you leave. And Trent"—he walked over and extended his hand, hoping it would break up the moment they were about to have—"it was great to meet you."

Trent pulled away from Jenna and glanced over at Dean. He nodded and shook Dean's hand. "Thanks for letting me crash on your sofa," he said.

Dean shrugged. "Of course. Anytime."

Trent turned his focus back to Jenna, and Dean realized that he was most definitely the third wheel in this situation. So he nodded—to no one in particular—and headed for the door. He was ready to focus on work.

He had to plan a Christmas party at the food shelf, make sure dinner was ready, and double check that they had enough supplies to give every kid a gift. This time of year was nice, though. Even though he had a lot of things to do, there was never a shortage of volunteers.

Sure they took time to train, but they were eager and willing to show up.

Dean climbed into his car, and before he knew it, he was at Humanitarian Hearts. He turned off his car and climbed out. Then he made his way to the back doors and unlocked them.

The kitchen was pitch-black, and Dean leaned over to flip on the lights. The back door shut after him with a thud, shutting Dean off from the rest of the world. He took in a deep breath as he walked across the floor and over to his office. He was excited to lose himself for a few hours before the staff came in to get started on breakfast.

After he caught up on his emails and checked his orders, the sound of the chefs setting up drifted through from the kitchen. He leaned back and raised his hands over his head, yawning.

Work was exactly what he needed to help him forget his feelings for Jenna. He'd already gone two hours without thinking about her.

It felt great, until her face flitted into his mind and, suddenly, reality hit him. He couldn't hide out in his office forever. At some point, he was going to have to return to his house and face the woman who'd ripped out his heart.

As much as he was trying to tell himself that he'd moved on…he hadn't. The same, familiar ache inside of his chest rose to the surface every time he thought about Jenna.

"Knock, knock," Nancy's voice rang out as she rapped her knuckles on his door.

Dean straightened, clearing his throat. "Yep," he said, nodding for her to come in.

"We have a volunteer who wants to say hello," Nancy said as she raised her eyebrows.

Dean's heart began to pound in his chest. Was it Jenna? Had she decided to come here and ditch Sondra's Christmassy plans for the day?

A woman with blonde, curly hair and a wide smile stepped

into his office. At first, Dean wondered when Jenna had had time to change her hair, but then realized that it wasn't Jenna who was standing there, but Naomi.

"Hey, Dean," she said, raising her hand in a wave.

Dean blinked. He glanced over at Nancy, who was staring at him as if she were willing him to say something.

"He's normally not this tongue-tied," Nancy said as she smiled at Naomi.

"I'm okay," Dean said, standing up and reaching across his desk. He held his hand out and then realized that Naomi was a good five feet from his desk.

Feeling like an idiot, he rounded his desk and stepped up to her. "Sorry, I've been so distracted with the Christmas plans that my mind is somewhere else."

Naomi smiled as she tucked her hair behind her ear. "I'm so sorry. I shouldn't have interrupted."

"You're not interrupting," Nancy said as she made a point to stare at Dean.

"Nancy's right. You're not interrupting." Dean forced his smile to widen to drive the point home.

Naomi smiled up at him. Her lips were tipped up slightly, and she was studying him through her thick lashes. Which was strange—Dean wasn't the kind of guy who noticed women's eyelashes.

He cleared his throat and glanced over at Nancy, who was grinning like a fool. Realization dawned on him. She was attempting to set them up.

Dean distracted himself by fiddling with the papers on his desk. An awkward silence settled in the room, making Dean twitch. He needed to speak before he went insane.

"So, are you volunteering here?" Dean asked.

"I thought she could help with organizing the Christmas party. You know, sort of be your right-hand man?" Nancy said as she stepped forward.

Dean glanced over at her. He wasn't sure what she meant. He normally flew solo. "A right-hand man?"

Naomi nodded. "Only if you need it. I overheard Nancy talking to my mother about how stressed you've been, and I offered to help. I'm extremely detail-oriented, and I'd hate to see you doing this all by yourself."

Nancy was grinning from ear to ear. "You always say that you never get to enjoy the holiday season because you're so swamped here. With Naomi helping out, you'll be able to spend more time with your family. Maybe go out for an evening."

Dean did not like the way Nancy was wiggling her eyebrows. Or the hint to her tone. But, what she said did have some truth to it. He wore himself out every year planning the food shelf's Christmas party. What could it hurt to have Naomi take some of that burden?

"Are you sure this is what you want?" he asked.

Naomi nodded. "More than anything," she breathed out.

Dean furrowed his brow but then decided to ignore her strange reaction. "Awesome. Nancy, can you run her through the safety precautions video to train her in?" He turned to Naomi. "Once you've completed that, I have a stack of things for you to do."

Naomi nodded, her cheeks flushing as she stepped forward. "Thanks for taking me aboard," she said and then giggled.

"Of course. Happy to have you here."

7

JENNA

Jenna was squished. She was sitting between Tiffany and Beth at her mother's quilting table. They were tying Christmas quilts to give away at Dean's work—a Braxton family tradition. Which, in years past, hadn't been this crowded. But with five women crowding around the table, Jenna was beginning to feel claustrophobic.

"I'm sorry," Beth said as she began to scoot her chair away from the table. "This baby is killing my lung capacity. I swear, she's content to reside inside my rib cage instead of where she belongs." Beth leaned her head back and extended her legs out as she took a deep breath.

"I definitely don't miss that," Layla said as she bent down to coo at Penelope, who was sitting in her car seat next to her.

"James was my mover and my biggest baby," Sondra piped up as she shoved her needle into the quilt. "But Jackson wasn't too far behind him." She raised her gaze and zeroed in on Isabel.

Isabel paled and Jenna realized exactly where her mom was going with this. From Isabel's reaction, Jenna knew she needed to swoop in. "Trent left this morning," she blurted out.

All eyes turned toward her.

Sondra parted her lips as she stared at Jenna. "What did you do?"

Jenna scoffed as her shoulders instantly dropped. Of course, her mother would assume she'd done something wrong. For a brief moment, she considered playing along, but then she decided against it. "He's filling in for someone who got his kids for Christmas. He's headed to Paris," Jenna said as she shoved in the needle and pulled the yarn through so she could tie it.

"Oh, that's a good man right there, Jenna," Sondra said as she shook her finger in Jenna's direction. "You make sure you do everything you can to hold onto him. Plus, it would be nice to have a pilot in the family."

Jenna resisted the urge to tip her head back and sigh. "I will, Mom."

"I mean, you have a reputation, dear. Use your brothers as inspiration. They've found lovely wives and are doing what people who are in love should be doing—having babies." Sondra adjusted the readers on her nose as she stared at Jenna.

Isabel stood and excused herself. She looked sick as she scrambled to leave the room. Jenna glanced back at her mom, hoping Sondra didn't notice. Something was up with Isabel, and she didn't want her her mother's hawk-like senses to pick it up.

"You're right," Jenna hurried to say. "I should work harder on my relationship with Trent. After all, I only have so many eggs."

Sondra had begun to turn to watch Isabel, but she stopped and focused back on Jenna. "Right. That's what I've been saying. It's important for you to focus. You've had your schooling, now it's time to think of your future family." Sondra reached down to grab her glass of iced tea and took a sip.

A desire to go after Isabel rushed through Jenna, so she stood, declared that she needed to go to the bathroom, and hurried out of the room. It took a few minutes, but she finally found Isabel sitting on the back porch, hugging her knees and rubbing her eyes.

Jenna's heart went out to her sister-in-law as she grabbed a nearby rocking chair and scooted it over. Isabel's eyes went wide as she shifted around on her seat. She wiped at her cheeks and forced a smile.

"Sorry about that. My mother can be ruthless sometimes," Jenna said as she settled down on her chair.

Isabel was tense at first, but then Jenna watched as her shoulders began to sag and a defeated expression passed over her face. It was all Jenna could do to not reach out and hug her sister-in-law who looked like she was holding the world on her shoulders.

"Wanna talk about it?" Jenna asked, hoping that she wasn't going to scare her off.

Isabel blinked a few times and then sighed as she stared off toward the garage. Silence engulfed them, but Jenna remained quiet. This was Isabel's time. If she needed to take more of it, then Jenna would let her.

"We lost a baby last month," she whispered. She sounded as if she were choking out the words.

Jenna's heart dropped. "Oh, Isabel, I'm so sorry."

Tears were streaming down Isabel's face. She wiped them away, choking back her sob with a laugh. "I was only a few months along. Half the time I didn't even know I was pregnant." She sniffled as she cleared her throat. "I had this foolish hope that it was a gift from my dad. That, somehow, he was sending that baby to us." She closed her eyes for a moment. "Is that silly to think?"

Jenna studied Isabel. She wanted nothing more than to reach over and take away the pain that Isabel was feeling. It had to be a lot, losing her dad and a baby in span of just a few months. "No," she whispered. "I don't think that's crazy at all. I believe your dad is looking down on you right now." Jenna reached over and rested her hand on Isabel's.

Isabel hesitated. "You're such a sweetie. Thanks for not thinking that I'm a blubbering mess."

Jenna smiled over at her. "How's Jackson taking it?"

Isabel shrugged. "I don't know. He doesn't really talk about it. You know him. He's a problem solver, and this is a problem he can't fix." Her lip began to quiver as if she were moments away from breaking down again.

"He'll come around. I know he will."

Isabel nodded. "I know. He's just treated me like I'm made out of glass ever since Dad died. Like he's worried I'm going to break from a single touch." She sighed as she zipped up her hoodie and wrapped her arms around her knees. "I just wish he would talk to me."

"He's not talking to you?" Jenna asked—probably a bit too loud.

Isabel shushed her as she looked around. "Not like that. He just skirts around the topic of the baby and dad. I try to tell him that I'm okay, that I need to talk about it, but he's withdrawn." Isabel forced a smile. "But please don't tell him I said anything. I would hate for him to think I was gossiping or something."

Jenna sat there with her lips parted as she studied Isabel. She had half a mind to march over to the gun range where her dad and brothers were having a guys' afternoon and give her brother what for.

Jackson was sweet, but he could be dense. Him withdrawing himself because he felt that it was the right thing to do for Isabel wasn't a surprise. But it did irritate her to no end.

Isabel shivered as she set her feet down on the porch. "I think I'm going to go take a nap. Can you tell your mom that I'm upstairs? I really don't want her to catch me like this." Isabel drew a circle around her face.

Jenna nodded. "Of course. I'll keep her distracted."

Isabel looked grateful as she blotted her eyes and sniffled. "Thanks, Jenna. You're a great friend."

"Anytime you want to talk, I'm here." Jenna smiled, hoping Isabel would pick up on her sincerity.

"I know," Isabel said. She padded across the porch and pulled open the back door.

Jenna rocked back in her chair for a moment. She took in a few deep breaths as she glanced up toward the blue sky. The air was crisp for South Carolina. The weather forecaster said it was unseasonably cold for this time of year. He also predicted that there might be snow for the first time in years.

Jenna folded her arms across her chest and slipped her feet to the floor. She needed to prepare herself to go back into her parents' house and face her mother down. Again.

After she pulled open the back door, she found Sondra standing in the kitchen, next to a kettle that was hissing. Sondra ran her gaze over Jenna and turned her focus back to the cupboard. She pulled a few mugs down and set them in front of her.

"Everything okay with Isabel?" Sondra asked, her back still facing Jenna.

Jenna blew out her breath and nodded. "Yeah. She's just tired. She told me to tell you she's taking a nap." Forcing a smile, Jenna walked over to stand next to her mother.

Sondra was a bloodhound for stressful situations. If she sensed for even a moment that something was wrong with Isabel, she would do her darndest to figure out what the problem was.

Jenna cared about her brother and sister-in-law. They didn't need Sondra telling them that everything was going to be okay, that they just needed to pick themselves up and try again. Isabel was mourning, and she needed space to mourn.

"Can I help?" Jenna asked.

Sondra glanced over at her and nodded. "I'm making some apple cider to drink while we finish. Can you grab the packets in the cupboard over there?" Sondra nodded toward the pantry.

"Sure," Jenna said.

They worked in silence, Jenna filling the mugs with the powder and Sondra following with the hot water. Once all the mugs were steaming with the hot cider, Jenna helped her mother carry them out to where Layla and Tiffany were still sitting at the table. Beth was standing near the window with her hands on her back, swaying back and forth.

"Everything okay?" Jenna asked as she handed a mug to Tiffany.

"Thanks, and yeah, she's fine. She just said her lower back is killing her." Tiffany blew on the hot cider.

Jenna nodded as she walked over to Layla and handed her a mug. "Is this baby going to be a Christmas baby?" Jenna asked, smiling over at Beth.

Beth closed her eyes and shrugged. "I'm not sure I'm ready, but with the pains this girl is giving me, I think I'm okay with sooner rather than later."

Tiffany stood up quickly and ran from the room. Startled, Jenna glanced over at her, but before she could register what was happening, Tiffany was gone.

"My goodness, what was that about?" Sondra asked as she stood next to the table with raised eyebrows.

Layla set her mug behind her and was reaching down to pick up Penelope, who was cooing in her car seat. "She said she wasn't feeling too good," Layla said, a smile spreading across her lips as she held her daughter up in front of her.

Sondra clicked her tongue. "I do hope that she's not sick. That's the last thing we need. A whole houseful of vomiting relatives."

Jenna sighed as she slumped in her chair. "I'm sure it's nothing. If Tiffany was really sick, she wouldn't be here." But just to make sure, Jenna took her time sniffing the cider. If it had gone rancid, she didn't want to meet the same fate as Tiffany.

But it smelled like cinnamon and allspice, just like she

remembered. She parted her lips to blow on the cider and then slowly tipped some into her mouth. Her whole body warmed as she swallowed it.

She drank half the mug before she set it down by her chair and returned to the quilt. Sondra had declared that she needed some grandmother time with Penelope and whisked her from Layla's hands. She then danced Penelope over to the tree, pointing out all the ornaments.

Now alone with Beth and Layla, Jenna glanced up. Beth was still standing by the window, swaying, while Layla hunched over the quilt, tying the strings she's just sewn.

Jenna couldn't help the smile that emerged on her lips. Growing up the only girl of the Braxton kids, she'd always dreamed of holidays just like this. Girls huddled around the quilting frame, talking and laughing.

She was grateful that her brothers had found such sweet wives and couldn't wait to spend a lot more holiday's just like this.

They finished tying the quilt and then worked on the binding for the other quilts in the corner. By four in the evening, all the Braxton men came tromping back into the house, laughing and boasting about who shot the best.

Isabel had come back down, and Tiffany was looking a lot better. James scooped up Penelope in one arm and wrapped his other arm around Layla. Josh was working out knots in Beth's back, and Jordan ran around the living room until Jimmy boomed out for him to sit down.

Realizing that she was the only one without someone, Jenna felt a desire to leave. She loved her family, but without Trent there, she realized how lonely she felt.

"Will you be a dear and run these quilts down to Humanitarian Hearts?" Sondra said as she sidled up next to Jenna. "While you're there, you can peel Dean away from work and bring him back here for dinner. I have a ham in the oven that'll be ready in a few hours,"

Desperate to get out of the house, Jenna nodded before she fully realized what she'd agreed to. It wasn't until all the quilts were loaded into the back of her rental and she was sitting in the driver's seat that she realized she was on her way to see Dean.

The morning had been too comfortable. Sitting in the kitchen, watching him cook breakfast for her. She'd completely forgotten about Trent until Dean reminded her he was there.

She hated herself for feeling so at home around Dean. Like he was the only one who understood her. He was the only one who knew the pain of growing up a Braxton.

Not to mention that every time she saw him, she was instantly transported back to the summer. Back to their kiss.

Clearing her throat, Jenna shoved her key into the ignition and turned it, causing the engine to sputter to life. She pulled out of the driveway and threw the car into drive.

Thinking too much about a kiss that could never happen again would get her in trouble. She needed to decide right now that she was over Dean. After all, she was lousy at relationships, and dragging Dean into one of her failures wasn't what she wanted for him.

He deserved someone who he could depend on, and that wasn't Jenna. If she ever began to doubt that, all she had to do was look at her parents' Christmas tree.

Jenna Braxton and *happily ever after* didn't go hand in hand. Despite how much her mother wanted her married and popping out babies, Jenna doubted that it was even in the cards for her.

Before she knew it, Jenna was pulling into the parking lot of Humanitarian Hearts. Blowing out her breath, Jenna idled in the parking spot, the exhaust billowing around her. Then, feeling like an idiot, she turned off the engine and climbed out of the car. If she was moving past Dean, she could see him. Talk to him. Like a normal human being.

It was the first step in proving to herself that she didn't care about him. That Trent was the man she loved.

Jenna slammed the driver's door and hurried across the parking lot to the front door. Warmth enveloped her as she stepped into the dining room. A few people were sitting at a table, sipping on coffee and eating cookies.

Jenna nodded at a few of them who raised their heads as she walked by. Once she was through the dining room and into the kitchen, she headed over to Dean's office. But the sound of female laughter caused her to stop in her tracks.

She listened, her ears perked. Who was in there? Jenna rubbed her temples. It wasn't unusual for Dean to talk to women. After all, he had quite a few female volunteers and employees. And why did she even care? She was with Trent. Dean was free to date.

When bile rose up into her throat at the thought of Dean dating, Jenna cleared her mind and decided to focus on what she was there to do. Dean was just the receiver of the quilts. Well, she also needed to invite him to dinner. But that was all.

She only had platonic feelings for Dean. She loved him like a brother, nothing more.

So she took a deep breath and focused her mind as she stepped around the corner and into Dean's office.

8

DEAN

Dean wasn't quite sure what was going on. Naomi had finished the project he'd given her to sort out the strings of lights and replace any missing or burned out bulbs. And she'd done it in record time, which he was grateful for.

There was a lot of work to do, and the fact that Naomi was speedy and thorough meant there was less for him to worry about.

But now she was practically sitting on his desk, asking him about the spreadsheets he was working on. He'd originally thought she was genuinely interested, but he didn't think that anymore.

Every time she moved, it seemed like she was making a point to brush her hand against his, or her arm against his shoulder. He had no interest in Naomi that way, but he couldn't help wondering what her game was.

"Knock, knock," Jenna called out.

Dean didn't have enough time to react before Jenna stepped into his office. Her cheeks were flushed, but when her gaze ran over Naomi, her skin paled. She cleared her throat as she straightened, and Dean fought with himself to not push Naomi off his desk.

He could only imagine what Jenna was thinking, and he didn't want her to think those things at all.

"Jenna," Dean said, pushing his chair out as he stood. That was the quickest way for him to get away from Naomi, who remained rooted on his desk.

Jenna's lips tipped up into a forced smile as she glanced over at Naomi and then back to Dean. "I'm sorry. You're busy. I can come back later," she said as she turned to leave.

"Wait," he said, stepping around his desk and raising his hands. "Naomi and I were just wrapping up." How could he say the things he wanted to say without making things awkward? Nothing he was coming up with was helpful at all.

"Right," Naomi said as she slipped off his desk, adjusted her pencil skirt, and wandered over to Jenna. "I'm Naomi, Dean's right-hand man. And you are?" she asked, reaching her hand out.

Jenna glanced down at Naomi's waiting hand. Then she shook it. "Jenna. Dean's...sister."

Ouch. That hurt to hear.

"Oh, nice to meet you." Naomi leaned toward her. "You don't look like Dean."

"Foster sister," Dean interjected. Call him crazy, but Jenna classifying herself as his sister almost delegitimized what had happened between them over the summer. It negated the feelings he had for her. It wasn't until this moment that Dean realized he hated the word sister.

Naomi glanced over at Dean with her lips parted as she slowly began to nod. "Foster sister. Oh, that means you're a Braxton," she said.

Jenna nodded, a bit too fast. "That's right. I'm the youngest." She pushed her hands through her hair. "I'm here to drop off the quilts we made." She raised her eyebrows and then turned.

"I'll go get them," she said as she practically sprinted from the room.

"Wait," Dean said as he followed after her. But as he stepped out into the kitchen, the only sign of where Jenna had gone was the swinging door.

"Do you need my help?" Naomi called after him, but he was through the kitchen and out into the dining room before he could respond.

Regret. Frustration. Anger. All of those feelings were coursing through Dean as he followed after Jenna. She was grabbing something from the back seat of her car when he got outside.

He crossed the parking lot and stood next to the car, waiting for her to emerge. When she did, she had her hands completely full of blankets. Without even thinking, Dean stepped forward and wrapped his arms around them. Just as he did, his hands brushed her, and jolts of electricity shot up his arms.

If Jenna had prepared a reason why he couldn't help her, she must have forgotten it. Because, despite her lips being parted, she just dropped her arms, unloading the blankets into his.

"Thanks," she murmured as she disappeared again. When she reemerged, she had about half the amount of blankets as the first load. She stepped away from the car and kicked the door closed.

"Wow. You guys worked hard," Dean said as he allowed a teasing smile to emerge.

Jenna peeked over at him for a second before she started making her way across the parking lot. "We didn't do all of these today. Mom did some with the ladies from church last week. We just finished up what was left."

Dean quickened his pace so that he could help pull open the door. As he held it for her, Dean studied her, hoping she'd look over at him. But she didn't. Instead, she barreled into the building like a woman on a mission.

Dean stifled a sigh as he realized he was a hopeless fool. Why did he think Jenna would change her mind? After all, she'd brought a guy home to meet her family. She'd *told* him that she wanted nothing to do with him.

She'd all but physically shoved him from her life. What was it going to take for him to get the hint? He needed to accept that they weren't going to happen.

Jenna was staring at him as if she were expecting him to do something. Dean nodded toward the kitchen door. "Through the back. We can put them in the storage room until the Christmas party."

Jenna glanced in the direction that Dean had motioned and nodded. "Perfect. Let's go."

Dean followed after her. When they got to the storage room, Jenna found an empty table and set down the blankets. Then she began to refold the ones that had come undone. Not wanting to miss out on time with Jenna, Dean set down his blankets and did the same.

"So, are you sad?" Dean asked when he couldn't take the silence anymore. When his question hit his ears, Dean winced. Why would he ask that?

Jenna was studying him as she folded. "About what?"

Dean cleared his throat and found an empty shelf to stick his folded blanket on. "That Trent left."

Jenna grew quiet as she waited for Dean to step aside. When he did, she placed her blanket on top of his. "I'm not sure sad is the right word."

Dean tried not to feel elated. Like, somehow she was telling him she didn't care for Trent like he was dreading she did.

"What about you? Are you excited to have Naomi working with you?" She kept her gaze focused on the blanket she was folding. As if she too was worried what Dean's reaction might be.

"Excited? I'm not sure that's the right word, either." He

grabbed another blanket. "Nancy kind of sprung it on me a few hours ago. But it's been helpful. There's a lot of things to get done every day, and not enough hands to do them."

Those words had never rung truer. Half of the time he was overwhelmed with his work at Humanitarian Hearts. Ever since Jackson swept Isabel out of Honey Grove, he'd been down someone he could count on.

Since the job didn't pay a whole lot, he was having a hard time finding anyone that wouldn't leave at the hint of another job.

"I can help," Jenna said as she turned to slide the blanket she'd folded next to the stack that already filled the shelf.

"You what?" Dean asked, leaning forward.

Jenna blew out her breath as she turned to face Dean. Her eyes were wide, and she had a no-nonsense look on her face. "I can help. I'm here anyway. Plus, it'll give me a break from Mom." Jenna dabbed her forehead with her wrist as she glanced around the room. "You need the help, and I have the time."

Still shocked that Jenna was offering to help him, Dean began to nod. "Um, okay. Yeah, that would be great." He tried to muscle down the excitement that was rising inside of him. "Do you want to start tonight?"

Jenna studied him and then nodded. "Sure. Mom wants us home for dinner. Ham this time. But I can help until the very last minute."

Dean began to fold faster, placing the last few blankets onto the shelf. "Well, awesome. Yeah, that would be really helpful." He stood next to her, staring down at her big brown eyes. So many memories came rushing back to him, and despite his best efforts, they settled inside of him.

For a moment, he allowed himself to remember what it was like to love Jenna. To hold her next to him. It was a feeling he longed for so deeply and poignantly that it was hard to convince his body and his soul that he couldn't have it. Even when she was so close to him that he could reach out and touch her.

He savored the feeling of standing next to her for a moment more and then extended his hand and nodded toward the door. "Come on. You can get started out here. Nancy can get you suited up. I heard her cursing the carrots earlier, so I'm sure she'll put you on chopping duty. It's minestrone tonight."

Jenna blinked a few times, as if she were under the same spell Dean had been. She nodded and walked out the door. Now alone, Dean pushed his hands through his hair as he tipped his face to the ceiling.

What was he doing? Man, he was a glutton for punishment. He needed to get his head on straight if he was going to survive this holiday season.

When he got out to the kitchen, his gaze instantly found Jenna. She'd pulled back her hair and was looking at Nancy, who was talking to her. Just as he'd predicted, Jenna had an apron on and a knife in her hand.

Dean dropped his gaze as he walked into his office and almost audibly groaned when he saw Naomi was still there. She was sitting on one of the chairs across from his desk and scrolling through her phone.

She must have heard him because as soon as he walked in, she dropped her phone and turned. "Everything okay?" she asked as she tucked some of her hair behind her ear.

Dean nodded. "Yep. Jenna was just dropping off some blankets to pass out for Christmas." He studied his desk for a moment before he sat. "I think we're done for today if you want to head home." He glanced up at Naomi and smiled.

Naomi parted her lips. "Are you sure? I can stick around if you need me."

Dean shook his head. "I think I'm good. I'm actually going to be heading out soon anyway."

Naomi stood, but didn't move to leave. Instead, she rounded

the desk and leaned against it. "Want to grab a bite, then? I've got nowhere to go, and you're leaving..." She raised her eyebrows.

"Right, but I have a Braxton dinner to get to. Sondra really values her family dinners around the holidays." He shrugged. "Raincheck?"

Naomi sighed as she straightened. "Of course. Well, I'll head out, then. Maybe tomorrow?"

Dean started to speak, but Naomi beat him to it.

"It's just family," she said. "You don't have to see them every night." Then she started making her way toward the door. "I'm sure they'll understand." She stood in the doorway and leaned back in. "What time do you want me here tomorrow?"

Would it be rude of him to say never? Her advances made him uncomfortable, so he didn't really want her hanging around here. Not when his feelings for Jenna were still so raw.

"Um, eight?" he said. He needed the help, and he would just need to tell Naomi that he wasn't interested in a relationship. Not now, and probably not ever.

Naomi winked at him. "You got it, boss!" And then she disappeared.

Dean leaned back in his chair as he sighed. This was going about as well as he figured it would. Being around Jenna had him all out of sorts, and adding Naomi to the mix didn't help.

"What will we understand?" Jenna's voice was quiet.

Dean snapped his gaze up to see her standing in the doorway with her knife clutched in one hand and a carrot in the other.

"What?" he asked.

"Naomi said we would understand. What would we understand?"

Dean reached out to fiddle with the mousepad in front of him. "She was talking about me missing a family dinner."

Jenna nodded slowly and then furrowed her brow again. "Why would you miss dinner?"

Dean cleared his throat. "Because we were going to dinner," he said, his voice drifting off with each word.

"Oh." Jenna grew quiet as she stood there. Then she stepped into the room, and Dean tensed. What was she doing?

"You should invite her tonight. I mean, I'm sure Mom would love to see you show up with someone." Jenna's smile looked forced, but Dean couldn't deny that she was suggesting he invite another woman to dinner. Like she was okay with it.

"Really?" he asked. He didn't want to invite Naomi to dinner, but he also didn't want to share that with Jenna. The last thing he needed was for Jenna to see through him. To know that he hadn't gotten over her. Not even a little.

Jenna snorted. "Of course. And with Naomi there, maybe the heat won't be on me and my singleness."

"Trent's just working."

A sad expression flashed across Jenna's face so fast that Dean wondered if he really saw it. But she shrugged and said, "True." So he decided he must have been wrong.

"Regardless, you should invite her. It would be nice for Mom to have someone to dote over."

Dean nodded as he rocked for a moment in his chair. "I'll think about it." He decided to focus on the stack of papers in front of him instead of Jenna, who was still standing in the doorway.

She raised the carrot and knife. "Gotta get back. These carrots aren't going to cut themselves."

Dean saluted her while keeping his focus on his desk. Once she was gone, he closed his eyes to focus his mind.

Jenna was thrusting him into the arms of another woman, and that didn't speak to her secretly pining after him. It spoke of a woman who had moved on with her own relationships.

It meant he was the only one sticking around for some

grandiose moment where Jenna would confess her feelings for him. A moment that was never going to happen.

Turning his attention back to his computer, he pushed Jenna and Naomi from his mind. He wasn't going to allow himself to be distracted by his feelings. Right now, he had a company to run. He didn't have time to decipher their conversations or decide what he wanted to do with either of them.

9

JENNA

J enna stood at the counter, her mind racing. She had so many thoughts and feelings about Dean and the conversation she'd overheard with Naomi, and none of them meshed with the determination she'd had when she drove into Honey Grove. The determination to convince herself that she was totally and completely over Dean.

"Yeah, right," she muttered under her breath as she glared at the carrots in front of her.

"You okay, honey?" Nancy asked, drawing Jenna's attention up.

Nancy was standing next to the stove, stirring a huge pot of soup.

Jenna pinched her lips together and nodded. She liked Nancy. She was sweet enough. But Jenna didn't really want to dive into her gigantic pool of failures with this stranger. The fewer people who knew about Dean and her, the better.

"Just tired. The holidays can do that to you."

Nancy snorted and nodded. "Don't I know it." Then she grew quiet. "It's been a long time since I've had a holiday like that."

There was pain in her expression that had Jenna furrowing her brow. "I'm so sorry." How could she have been so insensitive. Here she was, wallowing in her own self-pity about her stressful family life when there were people around her hurting.

"Oh, sweetie, it's not your fault. It's mine. I was the one who'd convinced myself that I didn't need anyone in my life. I was the one who focused on my career and pushed everyone away." Nancy sighed as she tapped the long wooden spoon on the edge of the pot and set it on the ceramic chicken that sat between the two back burners.

"You were never married?" Jenna asked as she reached forward and grabbed another carrot.

"I got close. Once." A warm smile spread across her lips. "His name was Peter, and he was..." Nancy leaned her hip against the counter and fanned her face.

Jenna laughed. "What happened to Peter?"

Nancy grew still as she focused on her clasped hands. Then she sighed and glanced up. "I pushed him away. Strange thing about pushing. Eventually, people leave."

Jenna could see tears start to form on the older woman's lashes. It pulled at her heartstrings, but what could she say? There was no way she could fix this for Nancy.

"Oh dear, I've brought you down." Nancy chuckled. Then she stepped forward and brought Jenna into a hug. "My story doesn't end badly. I'm happy. I've got this place and my quilting group. Plus my cat George." Then she winced. "I'm selling myself as a crazy cat lady, aren't I?"

Jenna laughed. Probably for the first time in a long time, she laughed with her soul. "It doesn't sound too bad."

Nancy nodded. "It's not." She pulled back and patted Jenna's hands. "There are just some days I wish I'd taken a different path, that's all." She sighed. "But, with life there's always decisions you are going to regret one day. Agency." Nancy rolled her eyes.

Jenna nodded as she brought over the cutting board full of carrots and dumped them into the soup pot. "What are you doing for Christmas?" Jenna asked.

Nancy was leaning against the counter with her legs stretched out in front of her. She had her arms folded. "I was going to serve dinner here and then head home to spend it with George. He gets cranky if I leave him for too long."

Jenna shook her head. "No. Not acceptable. You're coming over and spending Christmas with us." She shot Nancy a look that she hoped said she wasn't going to take no for an answer.

Nancy chuckled as she raised her eyebrows. "And I don't have a choice?"

"Nope."

The kitchen fell silent and then Nancy nodded. "If it's okay with Sondra, I'll come over. That sounds nice. Plus, I'd love to see Isabel again. She came in the other day with Jackson, but they hightailed it out of here before I could say anything."

Jenna clapped her hands together and smiled. "It's decided, then. You're coming."

Nancy smiled.

"Where's Nancy going?" Dean's voice drew Jenna's attention. He was leaning against the doorframe to his office. He had his hands tucked into the front pockets of his jeans. His hair, which was normally slicked back, had loosened from the day and was falling across his forehead.

Jenna's fingers itched to push it back like she'd done so many times in the past. Clearing her throat and her mind of those thoughts, Jenna turned her attention to the pot. She picked up the spoon and began to stir.

"Jenna invited me to Christmas dinner at the Braxtons," Nancy said.

"Oh, she did? That's awesome." Then Dean paused, and Jenna couldn't help but peer over at him. He was shooting Nancy an apologetic smile. "Sorry, I should have asked you."

Nancy waved him away. Then a mischievous smile spread across her lips. "You know how you can make it up to me?"

Dean straightened as he raised his hands. Intrigued, Jenna abandoned the spoon and turned, folding her arms across her chest.

"No. Nancy, no."

Nancy was laughing as she sashayed over to the under-the-counter radio and flipped it on. It took a few seconds for the CD to cue up, and suddenly *The Beautiful Blue Danube* began to play. Completely confused, Jenna watched Nancy waltz over to Dean.

"Nancy, no," Dean said again, but he was grinning.

"Oh, come on. We've danced before," Nancy said as she wrapped her hand around his wrist.

Dean's gaze slipped over to Jenna, and she couldn't help but smile. This was entertaining and exactly what she needed to move her focus from her failures.

Dean furrowed his brow and then sighed as he straightened and wrapped his arm around Nancy's back. Nancy giggled as they began waltzing around the kitchen.

"Last summer I wanted to take a dance class, you know, to get me out of my slump," Nancy said as Dean spun her around the room.

"Yeah?" Jenna asked.

"Dean graciously agreed to be my partner to help me practice. He's gotten pretty good if I say so myself," Nancy said as she glanced over at Jenna.

Jenna nodded. "You both are marvelous."

Nancy held her gaze for a moment before she pulled away. "Here, you should try. It really is exhilarating."

Jenna stared at Nancy and Dean. They had stopped in front of her. Nancy looked inviting, while Dean looked very uncomfortable.

"It's okay. I'm sure she doesn't want to dance," Dean said as he held up his hands.

Jenna knew she should have taken his resistance as a reason to back out, but for some reason, it made her angry. So despite the warning bells that were sounding in her mind, Jenna stepped up next to him.

Dean's eyes widened as he stared down at her, and Jenna could feel his body tighten. She felt a sense of satisfaction that Dean was uncomfortable standing next to her. It just proved to her that she wasn't the only one having issues. That, perhaps, he might still have feelings for her.

Nancy helped situate her hand in Dean's. Warmth enveloped her as Dean rested his hand on her upper back. She took in a deep breath, breathing in his scent. His woody, masculine scent. One she hadn't quite forgotten while she was gone.

It was a smell that she could fall into. It was comfort and excitement all wrapped into one.

Jenna was so engrossed in her heart-pounding and knee-weakening that she didn't notice Nancy had adjusted her hand on his upper arm and then patted her back.

"You let him lead, Jenna. I have a feeling you're a take-charge kind of gal, but with the waltz, you need to trust him." She pushed Jenna closer to Dean and then stepped back.

Jenna tried not to notice how excited Nancy looked as she stared at the two of them.

"Are you sure this is okay?" Dean asked. His voice was deep, and she could feel his stare. Her entire body was responding to his touch. It was scary and familiar at the same time.

"Yes," she whispered as she glanced up at him.

Dean held her gaze for a moment before he nodded and stepped forward—right onto her foot. Jenna yelped, and Dean winced as he moved to drop her arms.

"I don't think this is a good idea—"

"I'm fine. Let's try again." Jenna glanced up and hardened her gaze, hoping Dean would understand that she meant what she said.

Dean dropped his gaze to her. "Jenna, we don't—"

"I'm fine," she said again.

Dean paused and then nodded. "Listen to the beat. One, two, three. One, two, three." He moved forward, and this time, Jenna let her body relax and follow him.

Dean's hand tightened on her back, drawing her closer to him. Everything seemed to fade around them, and all Jenna could see and feel was Dean. His hand was warm as it held hers. His feet moved in time with the music, and Jenna couldn't help but follow him.

He was strong and familiar, and Jenna felt herself falling hard and fast. She knew she shouldn't. She knew she should walk away—running away would be smarter.

She'd already fallen for Dean once. She didn't think she could survive a second time.

"I'm going to spin you," Dean whispered. His voice was so deep that it sent shivers down her back.

"Okay," Jenna responded, glancing up.

Everything around her stopped moving. All she could see was Dean. His gaze was desperate, his brow furrowed as he focused on her.

Dean pressed on her lower back, and Jenna found herself spinning. All she needed was that small nudge from Dean, and she moved. Even though the last time she'd danced was in high school, it didn't matter. She trusted Dean, and she would follow where he led.

Jenna spun out and then back in. The momentum carried her through, and before she could stop herself, she rammed right into Dean's chest. Both his arms surrounded her, holding her against him.

Her hands were sprawled out across his chest. His warmth enveloped her, making it hard to breathe, to concentrate.

"Jenna," he whispered as he stared down at her.

Unable to stop herself, Jenna glanced up and met his gaze. It was so warm, so desperate. Every part of her body was responding to his.

And then, his gaze slipped down to her lips. For a moment, she allowed herself to remember what it was like to kiss him. To feel so completely at home in his arms. She almost let herself respond. To rise up and close the gap between their lips.

But she couldn't. Dean wasn't hers, and she couldn't be his.

"Nancy," she said as she pressed against his chest to push herself away.

Dean hesitated, tightening his grip on her, but then let her go. "She got a phone call and left a minute ago." His fingers traced the length of her back as he stepped away. He pushed his hands through his hair and looked at the floor.

Needing some fresh air, Jenna nodded and then speed-walked from the room. She needed to get as far away from Dean as possible. Before she did something stupid. Before she broke her heart and his for the second time this year.

She cared too much about Dean to treat him that way. If she wasn't going to give her heart to him, she needed to stay away. Dean deserved better than what she could give him.

"Jenna," Dean called after her, but she ignored him.

She didn't want to face him. Not now. She wasn't sure what she would say, and she knew that the things lingering on her tongue were things she shouldn't feel—couldn't feel. Not when she'd determined that she couldn't have Dean, and most certainly not when she was already with Trent.

Right now, she was the worst friend and an even worse girlfriend.

This was why she couldn't date anyone seriously. She failed at everything. And relationships were her Achilles' heel. She cared about Dean, so she would do the right thing and walk away.

In fact, if she cared about Trent, she'd walk away from him, too. He deserved better than what she was giving him. He was a genuinely good guy. He'd given up his holidays to help out a friend.

Jenna didn't deserve him.

She burst out into the cool evening air and made a beeline for her car. She was ready to let go of the tears that were clinging to her lids. She needed to cry as much as she needed to breathe.

She fumbled for her car keys, but her vision was blurring so much she couldn't find the right one. A sob escaped her lips as she tipped her face toward the sky and closed her eyes.

"Let me." Dean's voice startled her. She jumped back and glanced over to find him standing next to her, reaching for her keys.

"You don't—"

But Dean didn't look interested in hearing what she had to say. He took her keys and unlocked the door. Then he pulled it open.

"Do you need me to drive you?" he asked. His voice was deep and so full of caring that it frustrated her. She didn't deserve his love. She didn't deserve anyone's love. Not when she couldn't fully give herself to anyone.

"I'm okay. It's not too far." She sniffled as she swiped at her tears.

Dean nodded and then shook out her coat—she'd left it behind in her rush to get out of there. He held it up and raised his eyebrows at her.

Jenna slipped her arms into her jacket, and Dean pulled it up onto her shoulders. Then he hesitated, his hands lingering on her shoulders for a moment.

"I'm sorry," he said.

Jenna shook her head as she turned. "Don't say that. None of this is your fault. None of it has been your fault. It's all me." She forced a smile, hoping her face wasn't blotchy from crying. "You have been so good to me, and someday you'll find a girl who can love you fully."

Dean studied her with his brow furrowed. He glanced to the building and then back to her while shoving his hands into his front pockets. "Someday?"

Jenna nodded. And then just to prove to him that she meant it, she reached out and rested her hand on his upper arm. "You're a great guy."

He scoffed. "Thanks, Jenna." Then he focused back on her, his gaze betraying his words. There was a depth to his gaze. The way he looked at her had butterflies dive-bombing her stomach.

Realizing that this was not going to help either of them, Jenna just turned and slipped onto the driver's seat.

Dean stood in the parking lot as she started the engine and pulled out of the lot. She could feel his gaze on her as she took a left and turned down Main Street.

It wasn't until she was idling at the stoplight a block down that she allowed herself to glance up to the rearview mirror. He'd gone back inside. She let out another sob and finally allowed the tears to flow.

She really didn't know how she got home. For half the drive, she was wiping away the tears that spilled down her cheeks. But as she pulled into the driveway, she turned the engine off and sat in her car, staring out at the twinkling Christmas lights in front of her.

She could see the shadows of people moving around inside as they passed by the window. She didn't need to check her phone to know that her mother had called to ask where she was and why she wasn't home for dinner yet.

And she had every intention of heading in there. But right then, she needed to call Trent. She was a mess, and it wasn't fair for her to drag him through it. He deserved better.

She was going to break things off with him. He was just a

bandage on a gaping wound. One that needed to heal before she could even imagine asking anyone to come on this journey with her.

Fixing Jenna should be her number one priority. And that started tonight.

10

DEAN

Dean's phone chimed from his back pocket as he locked up the soup kitchen that night. He didn't have to look to know that it was Mama Braxton, texting him for the millionth time to ask him where he was. Dinner had started. Now he was missing dessert.

Dean had already written her back saying Humanitarian Hearts needed him, but she didn't seem to care. Instead, she was guilting him for not being there. For missing this precious family time together.

Which he knew he should care about. But after what had happened with Jenna, he really wasn't interested in spending time with the Braxtons.

He felt guilty about that, but his heart was bleeding, and he needed a break from all the holiday merriment and small talk. All he needed right now was a scotch and his couch—well, as long as Jenna wasn't there.

When Dean got to his car, he pulled out his phone and glanced down. To his surprise, Jenna had texted him. "I'm staying with Tiffany and Jonathan tonight. I hope that's okay. I'm feeling like they may need me."

Dean blew out his breath as he texted a thumbs-up in response and then threw his phone onto the passenger seat. He rested his hands on the steering wheel and pushed, pressing his back into the seat.

He glared at his car. This whole situation with Jenna was killing him. All he wanted to do was take her into his arms and hold her. To make her his, forever. And yet, she was so resistant to any of it.

There were moments when he thought she felt the same, but in that same instant, she'd pull back, shut down and turn away from him. It was killing him trying to figure out how to win her love. Especially when she seemed hellbent on moving on from him.

Dean leaned over and started the engine. He threw the car into reverse and pulled out of the parking lot. By the time he got home to his dark house, he didn't feel any better or have any solutions to his problems.

He had nothing. Zero. He was just as confused as he'd been when he got into his car.

It was freezing cold, and his scotch was calling his name, so Dean pulled on his door handle and climbed out. He pulled his jacket closed as he slammed the car door shut and bounded up the walkway.

His house was warm and quiet when Dean got inside. He flipped on the living room light and kicked off his shoes. Then he hung up his jacket and looked around.

If someone had to judge from the inside of his house, they wouldn't have guessed it was Christmas. He didn't have a single Christmas light or decoration at all.

Dean promised himself that he would get at least a small tree or a wreath tomorrow on his way to the soup kitchen. At least then, he wouldn't feel like such a Grinch.

Once Dean was sitting on his couch with the game on in front of him and a scotch in his hand, he finally felt his stress melt away. He leaned back and rested his head on the wall behind him.

It was a replay of a football game from earlier that week, but he didn't care. When he lost himself in a game, it was just about the only time he didn't think about Jenna. Or his feelings for her.

Crap. It wasn't working.

Taking another large gulp of his scotch, he settled back into his couch and focused on the screen. Just as he lost himself in the play, there was a knock on his door.

Confused, Dean set his glass on the side table next to him and stood. "Coming," he shouted.

Before he got to the door, it opened, and Jackson came walking in. Dean was startled at first but then smiled as he nodded at his friend.

"Well, just make yourself at home," he said as he took Jackson's hand. They pounded each other's backs for a moment before Jackson pulled back.

"Hey, man. You don't mind if I crash here for a bit?"

Dean shook his head as he made his way to the kitchen. "Scotch?" he asked not really waiting for a reply.

"Do you have to ask?"

Dean appeared in the doorway. "Nope. That's why I already have it."

He collapsed on the couch and then poured himself a glass. Jackson did the same thing. They drank in silence. They were both focused on the game, and it felt good, sitting next to his best friend. No need to speak. They could just exist.

"Isabel lost a baby," Jackson said.

Startled, Dean glanced over. For the first time that night, he realized how stressed Jackson looked. Dean felt like a jerk for being so focused on his own problems when his friend needed him.

"Man, I'm sorry," Dean said. It felt hollow. He wished he could offer more, but he didn't know what to say.

Jackson nodded as he took another sip. Then he rested his glass on his lap and shrugged. "It's just nice to be somewhere where I'm not getting lectured about the tax benefits of having children."

Dean nodded. That sounded like Sondra. "Did you tell her?"

Jackson shook his head. "Isabel's not ready." He scrubbed his face with his other hand. "She won't talk to me. After her dad died, I was so sacred I would lose her. And then with the baby..."

Jackson's voice drifted off. He took a deep breath and downed the rest of his scotch. He handed the glass over to Dean, who stared at it.

He wasn't sure if getting drunk was the solution to Jackson's problems, but then again what did he know? His last relationship resulted in him kissing Jackson's sister—something that would have earned him a death sentence when they were kids.

Who was he to give advice? So he took Jackson's glass, filled it up, and handed it back over. Silence engulfed the couch as they continued watching the game.

"What about you? Anyone in your life?" Jackson asked. He didn't turn his head, just tipped it toward Dean.

Dean was grateful for it. It was easier to talk when he wasn't being stared down. He took a minute to gather his thoughts as he brought his glass to his lips and took a drink. If he tried to tell Jackson what was going on, at some point he'd have to lie to his best friend. So he set his glass down, clapped his hands, and stood up.

"I need a pizza. Want a pizza? I'm going to order a pizza." He stood and made his way to the kitchen to find his phone.

"Pizza...wait—what?" Jackson's voice called as he followed him into the kitchen.

Dean tried not to groan as he grabbed his phone and typed

the name of the local pizza joint into Google Search. He pressed call just as Jackson moved to stand in front of him.

Dean brought his phone up to his cheek and heard the dial tone. He held up his finger, hoping that would deter his friend from asking any more prying questions.

"So there *is* someone," Jackson said as he leaned forward.

Dean pointed to his phone. "It's ringing—yes, hello," he said as a perky female voice sounded on the other end.

"Thanks for calling Fast and Quick Pizza, what can I get for you?"

Dean proceeded to order two cheese pizzas with a side of barbecue wings. Jackson said that he wanted some breadsticks, so Dean ordered those as well.

After he read off his credit card number, he debated keeping her on the line just to give him a reason not to talk to Jackson. But then he felt bad, so he thanked her and hung up.

Jackson looked poised to pounce. "Now are you going to tell me?" he asked as he folded his arms across his chest.

Dean sighed as he spun his phone on the countertop. "There's no one." And then Dean squinted. "Unless you consider Nancy as someone."

Jackson shook his head as he leaned against the counter. "I don't believe you."

Dean's stomach was turning, so he walked over to the fridge and grabbed some milk. After he poured and drank a glass, he turned to Jackson. "There was someone, but that's over now. Finished."

Jackson furrowed his brows. "Why? What happened?" Jackson raised his finger. "Did you bring her back to the house where happiness goes to die?"

Dean furrowed his brow. "My house is not a death house."

"Okay," Jackson said with what Dean felt was an unnecessary snort. "This house is lonely, man. I think that picture was here when you moved in." Jackson pointed to the sign above the light switch in the kitchen that read, *"I'm the best cook, just ask my grandkids."*

Dean scoffed and shrugged. "That's my favorite sign."

Jackson shook his head. "It's getting sad, man. You need a woman's touch in here. I mean, where's the Christmas cheer? If Mom saw the state of this place…" Jackson tsked.

Dean wanted to yell he was so frustrated. He *wanted* a woman's touch. A very specific woman. But she wouldn't give him a chance. And one of the reasons why was standing right in front of him.

And yet, there was nothing Dean could do about any of it. Jenna had said no. Repeatedly. It wasn't like Dean hadn't made an effort to show her that he cared. He had tried so hard back in the soup kitchen to show her how he felt. But she always brushed him off or ignored him. And there was only so much rejection a guy could take before he took the hint.

Jenna wasn't interested. Period.

"Well, I haven't met the perfect girl like you have," Dean lied.

Jackson's expression stilled as he studied Dean for a moment and then glanced up to the ceiling. "Yeah, I know."

Dean tapped his fingertips on the counter. "Then what are you doing here? At the house where, as you so lovingly said, happiness goes to die."

Jackson snorted and shrugged. "Sorry. That was a little harsh. It's a nice house. It's just…outdated."

Dean blew out his breath. "I know. I'm just waiting for the right girl to come along. Until then, I like my grandkids sign."

"All right, all right. But if you have a woman come over and she suddenly gets sick or has an emergency, you know what to change."

Dean nodded. "I'll take that sign down ASAP."

"Let's go watch the game. Isabel was sleeping when I left, and I could really use some pizza and sports. Mind if I stick around?"

Dean clapped him on the shoulder as they walked back into the living room. "Do you think I'd ever say no to you?"

They both collapsed on the couch.

"Yeah. You've always had a hard time resisting a Braxton plea," Jackson said as he handed his empty glass to Dean. "I'm going to grab a beer. I need something less heavy. Want one?" Jackson asked as he walked over to the small bar on the other end of the room.

"Nah. I've got to get some food in my stomach before I pump in any more booze."

Jackson nodded as he opened the fridge and grabbed out a beer.

A while later, a knock sounded at the door. He and Jackson had gotten sucked into the game, and Dean had lost all track of time. He glanced down at his watch, but he couldn't remember when he'd ordered the pizza. It felt a little too soon, though.

But maybe Fast and Quick Pizza was finally living up to its name. Dean stood and made his way over to the door and pulled it open. Naomi stood outside.

Confused, Dean glanced over to his driveway, but he only saw her car. And it wasn't sporting a Fast and Quick Pizza sign on the window.

"Naomi?" he asked as he dropped his gaze to her hands, which were shoved into her jacket pockets.

"Hey, Dean," she said, shooting him a smile.

Finally realizing that she wasn't there to deliver pizza, Dean felt like an idiot and stepped back. "Come on in." He didn't necessarily want her in his house, but he couldn't very well leave her outside in the cold.

"Thanks," she said as she ducked her head and stepped inside. Then she knocked her shoes against each other and adjusted her hair.

"Hey, Naomi," Jackson said as he stood slightly and waved.

"Jackson, hey." Naomi glanced at Dean. "Sorry to just drop by, but I tried calling and you didn't pick up."

Dean pulled his phone from his pocket and glanced down. "You did? It didn't come through."

Naomi pinched her lips together and nodded. Then she shrugged. "Huh, that's strange."

An awkward silence filled the room.

"Anyway, I was in the area, so I thought, what the heck, I'll just drop by."

"I'm gonna give you two some privacy. I'll be back," Jackson said as he shot Dean a look and then practically sprinted from the room.

That was strange, but before Dean could unpack it, Naomi spoke. "I was hoping to go to dinner tonight, but you never got back to me," she whispered as she peered up at him.

Dean cleared his throat and rubbed the back of his neck. "Yeah, sorry. I ended up working really late. I just got back, in fact. I'm waiting on some pizza now." Dean inwardly winced. He hadn't meant to say that. Hopefully Naomi wouldn't take that as an invitation.

"Oh, that's alright. I was worried I'd scared you off or something." Her smile felt syrupy sweet.

"No. Not scared."

Naomi stepped forward. "Good." She blew out her breath. Dean watched as the space between them quickly shrunk. "I'd really love to spend more time with you."

"You should come to Christmas dinner tomorrow," Jackson's proposal surprised both Dean and Naomi.

"She—what? Jackson, she probably has family." Dean shot her a sympathetic look as he shrugged apologetically.

"I don't, actually. My parents are at a photoshoot in Bali, and my sister is somewhere in the mountains of Colorado going by the name of Serenity. Besides the dinner at Humanitarian

CHRISTMAS IN HONEY GROVE   91

Hearts, I've got nothing going on." Naomi glanced at Dean. "If it's okay with you, I'd love to come."

Both Naomi and Jackson were staring at him. He swallowed, trying to come up with something to say other than, "sure." After all, he and Jenna were over, and if he turned down Naomi, he was sure Jackson would have some questions. Questions that Dean didn't want to answer.

So he did the only thing he could. He nodded. "That would be awesome. I'm sure Sondra would love for you to come."

Naomi's smile widened as she grinned over at Jackson. "Perfect. I can't wait."

Jackson collapsed back on the couch and rested a foot on the coffee table. "Just make sure you have a talent prepared. Isabel overheard Mom saying she may force a talent show on us tomorrow night after the Nativity play." Jackson flashed an annoyed look in Dean's direction.

Dean scoffed and rolled his eyes. "Well, that's just perfect."

Jackson shrugged, and the doorbell rang. Dean pulled open the door, this time revealing a pizza delivery driver standing on his doorstep.

"Great, I'm starving," Jackson said as he sat up and patted the coffee table.

After Dean signed the receipt, he thanked the man and shut the door, cutting off the cold draft that had rushed into the room.

With the warm boxes in his hands, he glanced over at Naomi, who was standing awkwardly in the entry.

Before he could give in to his desire to be alone with Jackson and sulk about Jenna, he shot Naomi a smile. "Hungry?" he asked as he nodded toward the armchair next to the couch.

Naomi's smile widened as she moved to unzip her jacket. "Starving."

11

JENNA

Jenna sat on a barstool in Tiffany and Jonathan's ridiculously massive kitchen. The enormous island in front of her was probably bigger than her apartment's entire living room. Tiffany was rummaging around in the freezer, looking for ice cream.

"I swear we have some in here," she said.

"I'll wait," Jenna said as she sniffled and grabbed a tissue from the box that Tiffany had given her.

"Ah, here it is," Tiffany said as she straightened and turned. She deposited a half-gallon of Moose Tracks on the white marble countertop.

"This house is amazing," Jenna murmured after she finished blowing her nose.

Tiffany sighed as she glanced around. "Yeah, Jonathan may have gone a bit overboard. But he wanted an amazing place to come home to when he's done playing for the season." Tiffany glanced around.

"Well, this definitely beats Mom and Dad's cramped house." Jenna spun around on the barstool, taking her time to survey the parts of the house she could see.

Tiffany snorted as she pulled open a drawer and set an ice cream scoop on the counter. Then she grabbed two white ceramic bowls from the cupboard above the dishwasher and set them next to the ice cream.

"You're joining me?" Jenna asked. She rested her elbows on the counter and leaned forward.

"I'm not leaving a sister alone. You just got dumped. I'm here for you," Tiffany said as she popped the top off the ice cream container and began to scoop.

"Well, I dumped him, but I'm not sure that makes a difference." A tear escaped, and Jenna took a second to wipe it away. Then she glanced up to her sister-in-law, who was studying her as she served up the ice cream.

"Doesn't matter. Solidarity, girl," Tiffany said as she raised her fist. Then she furrowed her brow. "Why did you dump him? Did he cheat on you?"

A rush of guilt ran through Jenna as the memory of her conversation with Trent spun through her mind. He'd been sad. Had wished she would give him a second chance. He said he should have never left and asked if she would wait to break up until he got back to the States.

But Jenna had held firm. The last thing she wanted to do was string Trent along, and honestly, that's what she had been doing. She didn't like the kind of person that had turned her into.

"No. It just wasn't going to work," Jenna said as she took the bowl of ice cream from Tiffany and picked up her spoon. The ice cream was cold and creamy. She sighed. It was just what she needed.

After barely holding it together through dinner, she'd jumped at the chance to leave with Tiffany and Jonathan when they declared they were heading home early. Tiffany hadn't been feeling well. Though, whatever had made her feel sick didn't seem to be bothering her anymore. Not when she was devouring ice cream by the spoonful.

Jenna chuckled as she took a few small bites. "Ever heard of brain freeze?" She nodded toward Tiffany's bowl.

Tiffany set her spoon down with a sheepish expression. "Sorry, I haven't been feeling good lately. This was the first thing in a long time that sounded good to eat." She wiped her lips with a tissue and stretched back on the stool.

"You've been feeling sick a lot lately?" Jenna asked as she studied Tiffany.

Tiffany nodded and lifted her spoon to take another bite. "It comes in waves, but it's been getting worse. I thought it was a bug, but I'm not running a temperature." She shrugged. "I'm chalking it up to stress. Your mom doesn't make the holidays easy."

Oh, there was so much to unpack there, but that wasn't what Jenna wanted to focus on. She leaned forward on her elbow and stared at Tiffany. Her sister-in-law leaned back with her eyes wide.

"What?" she asked around a mouthful of ice cream.

Jenna was giddy with excitement and had totally forgotten her ice cream. She raised a finger. "You're nauseous." She lifted another finger. "You're eating ice cream like a crazy lady." She lifted two more fingers. "You're tired. And I'm sure if I asked Jonathan, he'd say you're moody."

Tiffany narrowed her eyes as she stared at Jenna. Then, slowly, as realization dawned on her, her eyes slowly began to widen. "What? No. You don't think...?" She glanced around, her lips parted. Then she stared back at Jenna. "But we've been careful."

Jenna wrinkled her nose. That was not what she wanted to be thinking about when it involved her brothers.

Tiffany laughed as she shrugged and took another bite of ice cream. "Sorry."

Jenna shrugged, grabbed her bowl, and decided it needed her

full, undivided attention. "So what are you going to do?" Jenna asked.

Tiffany let out a sigh. "I don't know, get a test, I guess." Then she flinched. She glanced over at Jenna with desperation in her gaze. "Promise me you won't say anything. I...Isabel's having a hard time, and I'd hate to push this in her face."

Jenna's heart ached for her sister-in-law. "I know, she told me earlier. I wish there was something I could do."

Tiffany nodded. "I know. So do I." She scooped up the last bit of ice cream and then rinsed her bowl in the sink. "Well, that surprisingly hit the spot," she said as she rested her hands on her lower back and stretched.

Jenna nodded as she finished her ice cream. It was surprising how easily she forgot her own tiny issues when she was dealing with Tiffany and Isabel's. In the grand scheme of things, her breakup felt puny next to what they were going through.

Exhaustion took over, and Jenna yawned. Tiffany motioned toward the large staircase that split the first floor in half. "Come on, I just finished decorating the guest room. I'm excited for you to see it. The bathroom shower has all different kinds of jets."

"Bless Jonathan and his football career," Jenna mumbled as she followed behind Tiffany.

After she took a very long and very hot shower, Jenna dressed in a pair of pajamas that Tiffany lent her and then crawled into bed. The down comforter surrounded her as she sunk into the fluffy pillows.

Jenna located the remote and turned on the most recent Hallmark movie. She pulled the blankets up to her chin and breathed out, letting all the stress of the day sink into the mattress.

Sure, tomorrow, she was going to wake up single. And sure, she'd had a moment with Dean that she couldn't forget. But she was turning over a new leaf. She was going to be more positive and happy. She was going to love herself more than she had in the past.

Even if her heart was aching for Dean, she was going to be stronger. He deserved someone who could love him fully, and right now, she wasn't that person.

And she wasn't sure how long it would take before she was.

———

The next morning, the sound of voices from the main level work her up. Jenna stretched out on the bed. She brought up her hands and rubbed her eyes. They felt like she had sand in them.

Going straight to bed after crying for a while wasn't the best plan she'd ever had. She just hoped that by the time she got to her mom's house, she looked chipper and happy. If not, Sondra would smell the breakup on her.

She wasn't up for going through another "what happened? why did he dump you? what didn't you do?" session with her mom. It was Christmas Eve. She wanted to celebrate the holidays and not think about her failing love life.

Pulling off her covers, Jenna set her feet on the ground and stood. She found a robe in the nearby armoire and wrapped it around herself as she padded down the stairs.

Tiffany was sitting at the counter, snacking on saltines, while Jonathan focused on the pan on the stove in front of him.

Tiffany must have heard her come down the stairs because she turned just as Jenna walked in.

"Good morning, sleepy head," she said. Her expression turned sour as she sipped on her glass of water.

"How are you feeling?" Jenna asked.

"We're pregnant," Jonathan exclaimed, loudly.

Jenna glanced over at her brother and smiled. "I know. I was the first to know." She shot him a look and he playfully scowled back.

"Well, I was the first to officially know," Jonathan said as he picked up a spatula and waved it in Jenna's face. "I bought her a test this morning, and it's official." He got a goofy look on his face. "I'm going to be a daddy."

Jenna lightly punched him in the arm and extended her arms out and waved her hands at him. "Bring it in."

Jonathan laughed and squeezed her before he pulled back. "Tiff says you dumped Trent?" He smiled. "Nice." He patted Jenna on the head. "My sister, the player."

Jenna swatted at him, and then dodged his retaliatory swat with the spatula as she sprinted over to the coffee bar at the other end of the island. She wasn't up for talking about Trent this early in the morning without some coffee in her.

After she had a mug in her hand, she settled in next to Tiffany. Her sister-in-law turned green and, a few seconds later, excused herself to the bathroom. Tiffany had her hand clamped to her mouth as she went.

"Poor girl," Jenna said as she followed Tiffany with her gaze.

When she turned back to Jonathan, his jaw was clenched as he stared at the eggs in his pan. "Yeah, I know. It's hard to see her this sick. I wish there was something I could do. I hate puking."

Jenna nodded. "Ditto."

Jonathan fell silent and then sighed as he picked up the salt-shaker. "We were talking about Trent."

Jenna let out a groan as she rested her forehead on her arm. "I don't want to talk about Trent. We're over. Done." She closed her eyes and reveled in the feeling of the cool marble under her skin. Until she felt the pat of Jonathan's spatula on her arm. She sighed and straightened up, glaring at her brother.

His brows were furrowed as he met her gaze. "You're really

okay? If not, I'll get James, and we can get on the first plane to find him."

Jenna shook her head and smiled. "I know, thanks. But I'm fine. If anything, I broke Trent's heart. Like always." She muttered the last two words under her breath.

Jonathan was still staring at her as if he were trying to figure something out. Jenna could see the questions he wanted to ask her rolling around in his mind. But she wasn't ready to talk about it.

She slipped off the barstool and grabbed a piece of bacon from the plate in front of Jonathan. He protested, but Jenna just turned and headed back upstairs. She was going to grab her clothes and hightail it out of there.

She needed to get back to Dean's to pick up her things and then rush over to her parents' house by nine so the festivities could start. If she was late, Mom would never let her live it down.

When she pulled into Dean's driveway, she took a deep breath. She'd hoped she would feel better after the drive to his place, but she didn't. Instead, she felt just as confused and frustrated as she'd been when she slipped out of Jonathan and Tiffany's house.

Preparing herself for what she might find, Jenna pulled open her car door and stepped out. She clutched her dirty clothes in her arms as she hurried up to the door.

If she was lucky, she might be able to get in and get dressed before Dean noticed that she was even there. Or maybe he'd already left for Humanitarian Hearts, and she could avoid a whole awkward interaction with him.

Just as she moved to try the door handle, the door opened, and a very groggy Naomi appeared in front of her.

Naomi's eyebrows rose as she ran her gaze over Jenna. She must have been as surprised as Jenna.

"Naomi?" Jenna asked.

Dean suddenly appeared behind Naomi with a startled expression. "Jenna? I thought you were staying at Jonathan's."

Jenna fought down the feeling of dread as she began to put the pieces together. Dean was here. Naomi was here. It was early morning. Did that mean...?

She blinked as she fought back tears. She knew she had no right to be upset that Dean was moving on. She knew that. But it didn't make it hurt any less. She was a fool to think that Dean might still have feelings for her.

Then, before she could drown in self-pity, Jenna pushed past Naomi and Dean, muttering an apology. She headed into his guest room and grabbed her suitcase, shoving her dirty clothes into it, and then zipped it closed.

Tears blurred her vision as she set the suitcase down and raised the handle. She pulled it behind her as she headed for the kitchen.

Dean was standing a few feet from her room, his hand pushed through his hair and a look of worry etched across his face. Naomi was nowhere to be seen.

But there was no way she wanted to talk about this with Dean. She knew she didn't have a leg to stand on since she'd come back with Trent. Dean had every right to date who he wanted. He didn't need to explain himself to her.

"I'll see you at Mom's," she said as she started to sprint past him, hoping she could get out to her car before Dean said anything.

But as she moved past him, he reached out and touched her arm. "Jenna, wait."

Jenna winced before turning to face him. "Listen, you don't owe me an explanation. You're free to date whomever you want."

Dean winced as he studied her. "Listen, Naomi wasn't...I mean, we did—"

Jenna raised her hand. "I don't need to know. You don't need to explain anything to me. You're free." Her last sentence came out quiet, and she hated that she couldn't mask how she was feeling. She was pretty sure she looked and sounded heartbroken.

"She came over last night. I invited her to stay for dinner—well, Jackson invited her to stay. She passed out on my couch, and I couldn't wake her. We slept in separate bedrooms." Dean stepped closer.

Jenna's breath caught in her throat as she stared up at him. She wanted to believe that what he said was true. She wanted to believe that Dean would be loyal to her—even if there was no rational reason for him to do that.

"You can date her, though," she whispered as her eyes filled with tears. She hated herself for caring so much. She hated that she couldn't do the right thing and let Dean go. He obviously felt like he needed to run things by her. Like they had some kind of agreement.

It shouldn't be that way, and if she cared about him, she'd move on.

Dean's jaw twitched as he studied her. Then he nodded and leaned even closer. "What if I can't?" he whispered. It was so soft, that Jenna wondered if she'd even heard it.

Jenna pulled her arm away and wrapped her fingers around her suitcase handle. She turned, cleared her throat, and focused her emotions. She was going to be strong. She had to be.

"I'm headed to Mom's. I'll see you over there." She kept her gaze on the floor in front of her.

Dean didn't call her back as she walked through the kitchen, into the living room, and out the front door. She set her suitcase in the trunk and then climbed into the driver's seat.

Once the engine was on and cold air was blasting from the vents, Jenna turned to look at the front door and wondered if Dean was on the other side. She wondered if his heart was breaking as badly as hers was.

Then she pushed that thought from her mind as she slipped the car into reverse and pulled out of the driveway. When she was officially out of view from Dean's house, she allowed her tears to fall.

It hurt, walking away, but it was necessary. He may not feel it now, but someday he was going to be grateful that she'd left. Jenna was sure of it.

Breaking off this thing between them was the smartest option for both of them. Dean deserved to be free.

DEAN

By the time Dean rolled up to the Braxton house later that morning, he was in a sour mood. He'd contemplated calling Nancy to tell her he'd come in this morning more times than he could count. Spending time with the Braxtons was the last thing he wanted to do. Not only did he have a horrible hangover, but he was also kicking himself for how he left things with Jenna. He'd told her the truth. There was nothing romantic between him and Naomi.

Naomi had passed out on his couch and had refused to wake up when he and Jackson tried to wake her. So he let her sleep off the pizza and booze. In the morning, when she'd finally rolled off his couch, he told her to get her shoes and get out—in the nicest way possible.

It was just his horribly dumb luck that Jenna would walk up just as Naomi was leaving.

He'd never forget the look on Jenna's face when she saw Naomi. Or the way she looked when he tried to stop her.

He wanted to tell her everything—he'd even tried—but Jenna didn't seem interested. Instead, she'd grabbed her suitcase and left. Taking his heart with her.

So, now he was standing in the Braxtons' living room with all the Braxton boys and their wives, trying hard not to stare at Jenna, who was dressed as Mary for the soup kitchen's Nativity play. It was torture.

"Stop moving so much, Jenna. You're going to make me poke myself," Sondra scolded as she fussed with Jenna's hem.

"Ma, I still don't understand why it matters. The play is only a few minutes long. Just enough time for Dad to read the story. What does the hem matter?"

Beth came around the corner, wearing an identical dress. She was playing the part of pregnant Mary. "Hey, if I have to wear this getup, so do you," Beth said.

Jenna shot her an exasperated look and pinched her lips together.

Dean could see her frustration in how she held herself and the adorable way her cheeks flushed. It was taking all of his strength not to pull her into his arms.

She was pushing him away. He knew that. He just wasn't sure why.

"So how did it go this morning?" Jackson asked through his fluffy, grey beard. He was playing the part of a wise man. He spat a few times, as if trying to remove the beard hair from his mouth, then he finally growled and pulled the beard down below his chin.

"I, um…it was fine. I got her jacket and shoes and showed her to the door," Dean said as he shrugged and shoved his hands into his front pockets.

Jackson raised his bushy, grey, pasted-on eyebrows. "I bet."

"What are we talking about?" Josh asked. He approached wearing a very similar outfit, but instead of a grey beard, his was white.

"Dean had a girl sleep over last night," Jackson said as he winked at Dean.

"Oh, wow. Do I know her?" Josh asked.

Dean glanced over at Jenna for a moment before he turned his attention back to Jackson and Josh. He cleared his throat and shrugged. It looked like Jenna's shoulders had tensed up as she turned an ear toward Dean.

He hated that this conversation was hurting her. If he could, he'd shut it down right now, but Jackson and Josh weren't interested in that.

"Her name's Naomi," Jackson said. "She's cute. Barbara's daughter?" He folded his arms and leaned toward Josh.

"Barbara owns the flower shop that did our flowers," Jonathan said as he approached. He was the third wise man, with an identical black beard.

"That's right," Jackson said.

"So do you like her?" Jonathan asked as he bumped Dean's shoulder with his own.

Dean shrugged. "I'm not...I mean, we're working together. I'm not sure I'm ready to make that kind of declaration."

Josh, Jonathan, and Jackson all exchanged knowing looks. They were reading more into what he'd said than Dean was comfortable with.

"We're here!" James called from the kitchen. Everyone turned.

Sondra shouted out a hallelujah as she stood and hurried into the kitchen. Penelope was playing baby Jesus.

"Where have you been? If we don't get moving, we're going to be late," Sondra said as she flitted around James and Layla.

"Sorry, Penelope had a blowout, so we had to give her a quick bath," Layla said. She looked tired but content as she moved around the kitchen, grabbing a mug and filling it with coffee.

"Well, that's fine, but we need to get you fitted for your costume," Sondra said.

"Actually, we were wondering if someone else could play Joseph. James was up all night with Penelope. He needs a nap,"

Layla said as she reached out and rested her hand on James's chest.

Sondra's expression was frustrated, but then she sighed and nodded. "I understand. I guess…Dean can be Joseph."

Dean perked up when he heard his name. "What?"

Sondra pointed at him. "Next to Jenna on the couch is Joseph's costume. Put it on and come out here so I can adjust it. We need to be out of here in fifteen minutes if we are going to help you set up at the soup kitchen." She sounded desperate, so even though Dean didn't want to play Joseph to Jenna's Mary, he didn't fight it.

He nodded, grabbed the costume, and headed into the bathroom to change as quickly as he could. When he stepped out, he wasn't paying attention and ran right into someone.

"Sorry," he said as he reached out to steady them. Jenna turned around. Her cheeks were flushed as she mumbled an apology and stepped to the side.

Dean shrugged and moved past her, zeroing in on Sondra. He was ready to get out of this cramped house.

Thankfully, Sondra declared the costume perfect and then proceeded to wave her hands around to round up the family. Dean slipped from the house as fast as he could and walked briskly over to his car. He really wasn't in the mood to ride with anyone.

He waited, his engine idling, while everyone filed out of the house and into their respective vehicles. Sondra was the last to emerge, with her cheeks flushed and her purse clutched in one hand while she prodded Jordan with the other.

Jordan was dressed as a donkey—a very unhappy donkey. Dean couldn't hear what the kid was saying, but he looked like he was complaining.

Thankfully, no one attempted to ride with him. He tried not to notice Jenna get into the back of Jonathan and Tiffany's car.

Once everyone was in, they started the slow procession to

Humanitarian Hearts. Dean drove behind Sondra and Jimmy, trying to calm himself down. He was agitated, and Jimmy wasn't the fastest driver.

He knew he shouldn't be irritated with the family that had so willingly let him into their life—but he couldn't help it. Being around Jenna and not being able to touch her was killing him.

He wanted the happiness that the other Braxton children had found—even if some were experiencing heartbreak right now. He wanted it. All of it.

What was the point of living a lonely life? Being with someone meant he was going to have ups and downs. That his heart was going to break. Jackson was proof of that.

Sometimes, things just don't go the way you thought they should. But having someone by your side means you can deal with the pain that loving someone brings. And he wanted that person to be Jenna. There wasn't anyone else that could fill her shoes.

He loved her. Wholly and completely. He wanted nothing more than to tell her how he felt. He'd take the wrath of Jackson or the frustration of the whole Braxton family for falling for their precious daughter.

He hadn't meant for it to happen, but he was sick of fighting it. Jenna was meant to be with him, and he was meant to be with her. There was no getting around it anymore. And he didn't want to. He was tired of walking around with this sick feeling in the pit of his stomach. He was tired of not trying.

He was going to put himself out there. He wasn't sure when or how, but he was going to let the world know that he loved Jenna. After that, he'd deal with the fallout. At least he'd know that he'd done everything he could to find the happiness that he craved.

Dean pulled into his parking spot behind Humanitarian Hearts. He was filled with determination. It felt great to finally make the decision to take charge of his happiness.

And for the first time since he kissed Jenna over the summer, he felt excited. The weight that was bearing down on him felt lighter. It was refreshing.

Dean pulled open the back door that led into the kitchen. He nodded at Nancy, who was directing all of the volunteers as they minced and diced and got Christmas dinner ready for the ovens.

Nancy smiled and waved at him and then motioned to his costume. "Looking good," she said.

Dean shrugged. "I get to play Joseph."

She laughed and nodded.

Sondra wasn't going to be happy with Dean hanging out in the kitchen, so he strode out into the dining room. There were a few people already sitting at the tables. The meal started at one, and while they ate, the performance would begin.

Braxtons were milling around the room, waiting to be told what to do. Dean zeroed in on Jenna, who was standing with Layla and cooing at Penelope in her car seat. He began walking over to her, ready to confess everything, but stopped when Sondra stepped in front of him.

"Where are you going, Joseph?" she asked as she shook her forefinger at him and pointed toward the small stage that had been donated by a local party company. It was up against the wall on the other end of the room. Far away from Jenna.

Dean glanced down at Sondra. "What?" He hadn't been paying attention. He was focused on one thing—Jenna.

She pointed toward the stage. "Go. Beth's waiting to run through the beginning parts with you."

Dean glanced over to see that Beth was standing next to Jordan with her hand on her back. She looked exhausted, and Dean felt like a jerk for making a pregnant woman wait.

"Gotcha," he said, nodding to Sondra and making his way over to the stage.

An hour of practice passed before Dean finally got Jenna

alone. She'd excused herself to go to the bathroom, and Dean slipped away to confront her.

Sondra was talking to Jordan, who was complaining that his feet hurt and that he didn't want to play the donkey. She was in full lecture mode with him, so she didn't notice that Mary and Joseph had disappeared.

By the time Dean got to the bathrooms, no one was around. Jenna must have already gone in. So Dean leaned against the wall with his legs crossed in front of him. He'd just wait until she came out.

A few minutes later, Jenna emerged with an irritated expression on her face. She was muttering something under her breath as she adjusted the fabric of her dress.

"Everything okay?" Dean asked, his heart pounding in his chest as his mind swirled with anticipation. He thought he knew what he was going to say, but standing there, in front of Jenna, his tongue was tied, and he desperately tried to grab onto his previous plans.

Jenna yelped as she whipped around to face Dean. Her eyes were wide, and her lips were parted. "Geez. You scared me half to death," she said as she covered her heart with her hand.

Feeling sheepish, Dean straightened and stepped forward with his hand raised. "Sorry."

Jenna adjusted her dress again and shrugged. "It's okay." Then she furrowed her brow. "I should get back. If Mom finds both of us missing, she's going to kill someone." Jenna turned, and Dean did the only thing he could think of. He acted.

He reached out and grabbed her elbow, turning her around to face him. "Jenna," he said with desperation in his voice.

Jenna's body tensed before she turned her gaze up to meet his. "Dean, I—"

"Jenna, I know you think we can't make it, but I can't live like this anymore." He didn't want to interrupt her, but he knew if she spoke first, he wouldn't be able to say the things he wanted to say.

Jenna didn't move. Didn't part her lips to speak. And fear and worry began to creep into Dean's heart. Was he wrong? Didn't she care about him?

"Dean, I can't," she whispered. "Please don't ask me to."

Dean closed his eyes for a moment. "Are you happy?" he asked, the ball of emotions in his throat making it hard for him to speak.

Jenna furrowed her brow as she stared at him. "Does it matter?"

Dean studied her. "Yes. I can make you happy. Happier than Trent ever could." He knew her. More than any of the jokes she'd brought home to meet the family. He loved her. She had to see that.

"I broke up with Trent." She sighed and pulled her arm away from him. "Just like I would end up breaking up with you." Jenna wrapped her arms around her chest and gave him a forced smile. "It's better this way. You'll find someone else, I promise. I just…can't do what you want me to."

Dean stared at her. Was she serious? He was never going to find another woman he loved more than he loved her. She was his person. His soulmate. Everything in his life had led him to her. "Jenna, I—"

"There you two are. We can't have a Nativity set without Mary and Joseph." Sondra's voice startled them, and they turned to see Sondra walking up to them.

She held her hands out and was physically pushing them toward the dining room. "Come on. No time to dillydally. Food is being served, and we only have a few minutes before it's show time."

Dean cleared his throat and nodded. As soon as they were back in the dining room, Jenna peeled off, leaving Dean alone.

"You okay?" Jackson asked. He appeared next to Dean with two cups of juice and handed him one.

"Thanks," Dean said. He took the drink and downed it. "Yeah, I'm okay. It's just the holidays, man." Dean crumpled up the cup and shrugged.

Jackson was eyeing him like he didn't believe what he was saying, but then he just nodded and shrugged. "I took your advice."

Grateful for something else to talk about, Dean gave his attention to his friend. "You did?"

Jackson nodded. "When I got home last night, I talked to Isabel." Jackson's eyes teared up for a moment before he cleared his throat. "It was good. Apparently, she felt like I'd cut her off. That I was mad at her." Jackson's jaw twitched. "I told her that wasn't true." Jackson clapped Dean on the shoulder and smiled. "Thanks, man. Sometimes saying something is all you need to do. And I have you to thank for it."

Dean stared at Jackson as his words settled around him. He'd said something to Jenna, but it had been the wrong thing. He needed to say those three little words. The ones that told her the truth. How he really felt about her.

But before he could go find Jenna, Sondra came up behind him and pushed him to the stage. "We're starting, Joseph," Sondra hissed. Everyone in the completely full dining room quieted as Jimmy stood on the stage, reading from the Bible.

Beth and Jordan stood at the edge of the stage, waiting.

"What is going on with you?" Sondra asked.

Dean glanced down at her. "What do you mean?"

A sad expression fell over her face. "You're distant, like a lot of my children this Christmas." She smiled up at him, but he could still see the pain behind her attempt at happiness.

Dean moved to hug Sondra, but she just smiled and pushed him toward the stage. "It's time. Go."

Dean wanted to stay. He wanted to fix Sondra's sadness, but

there wasn't time. Instead, he nodded at Beth, who took his arm as they walked up the stairs together with Jordan braying behind them. That conversation was going to have to wait until another time, but it was going to happen.

Right after Dean told Jenna that he loved her, he was going to find a way to save this Christmas. If not for himself, then for Sondra.

She deserved it.

JENNA

Jenna was finding it extremely hard to concentrate as she watched Dean walk across the stage with Beth. They made an adorable Mary and Joseph on their journey to Bethlehem. Dean looked so caring as he smiled down at Beth.

It made Jenna's heart ache in a way she hadn't felt before. And Dean's words in the hallway rolled around in her mind like a marble she couldn't stop.

He cared about her. Still. After all these months. After she brought home another guy. After she told him repeatedly that she didn't want to have a relationship with him. He still cared.

Her heart swelled at that thought, and that angered her. She wasn't supposed to have feelings for Dean. Not when she couldn't act on them. Not when she knew that caring about him would inevitably hurt him. She couldn't be so selfish as to put him through that.

Dean had no family. The Braxtons were the only people in his life. What if they tried? What if Jenna let him into her life like she so desperately wanted to do?

What if it didn't work out? She couldn't ask her family and

Dean to pick. It wasn't fair of her to do that. To put the most important relationships in her life at risk like that.

If this Christmas had taught her anything, it was that family was most important. Everyone needed people in their life to love and cherish them. And if they didn't have that, what else was there?

"You okay?" Tiffany asked, startling her.

Jenna turned to see that Tiffany had stepped up next to her. She looked a little green as she wrapped her arms around her chest.

"Yeah, of course," she squeaked and then cleared her throat and settled on a nod. "Why?"

Tiffany gave her a sideways glance. "You just look really worried. Is it about Trent? Are you having second thoughts?"

Jenna pinched her lips and shook her head. At least with that she was completely confident that she made the right choice. "No. It was the right thing. I asked him to come for all the wrong reasons."

Tiffany nodded "Then what else is it? I haven't seen you this withdrawn in...forever." Tiffany stared at her as if she had the answer written on her forehead.

Blowing out her breath, Jenna just shrugged. "The holidays are hard, you know? Especially when you're single."

Tiffany reached out and wrapped her arm around Jenna's shoulders. She pulled her in tight. "I know, sweetie. And there's someone out there for you. I bet he's not as far away as you think. Heck, all it took was a weekend away for me to realize that I loved Jonathan."

Jenna smiled as she glanced over at her goofy brothers who were getting ready to climb the stage's stairs and act out the parts of the three wise men. "Yeah?" she asked.

Tiffany nodded. "It was scary, but sometimes, taking risks is what you have to do. If it were easy, everyone would be in love.

It takes someone who is brave. Who is willing to wear their heart on their sleeve for someone else."

Her expression softened as her hand found her stomach. "And when you realize that you're having a baby..." Her face flushed. "It's even scarier."

Jenna pulled her sister-in-law into a hug. "You're going to be a great mom. Seriously."

Tiffany blew out her breath as she studied Jenna. Then she nodded. "Thanks. Your confidence helps."

Jenna shrugged. "Any time." She grew quiet. "Can I ask you something?"

"Shoot."

"How did you get over the fear of starting a relationship with Jonathan? I mean, what if it didn't work out? You two were best friends. How did you get over that fear?" Jenna pinched her lips together when she realized that she was rambling. When she calmed her mind and glanced over at Tiffany, Tiffany's eyes were wide.

"Is there a friend you're interested in?" Tiffany's gaze began to comb the room.

Jenna reached out and grabbed her arm, hoping to distract her. "No. I was just wondering."

Tiffany chuckled. "I don't know. I guess I just realized that I could either be alone forever, or I could take the chance and create something with Jonathan." She sighed. "It's scary, risking something familiar for something unknown. But it's worth it." She wiggled her eyebrows. "He's mine. I don't have to worry about him finding someone else. Friends are friends until someone falls in love. Once Jonathan was married, there was no way we would have stayed so close.

"That's why I snagged him. I want him in my life. He's my best friend. I wasn't going to risk losing him because I was scared I wouldn't be able to make it work."

Tiffany's voice drifted off, and when Jenna looked up, she

saw that Tiffany's face was pale. She placed a hand over her face and quickly left the room. Just as she did, someone walked by with a plate piled high with ham.

Tiffany must have gotten nauseous from the smell, Jenna realized. She shot her sister-in-law a sympathetic look as she disappeared into the hallway that led to the bathroom. Now alone, Jenna glanced up to see that her brothers were just finishing the wise men part.

She was up next, so she made her way to the stage. She stepped up next to Layla, who was holding a sleeping Penelope.

"Ready for this?" Layla asked.

Jenna nodded and reached out. Layla laid Penelope into her arms. Instinctively, Jenna pulled Penelope to her chest and reveled in the warmth the tiny human put off.

"Ooh, that looks good on you," Layla said with a wink.

Jenna moved to speak, but Dean came up next to her, causing her whole body to warm. He said something to Layla, but Jenna couldn't hear anything over the pounding of her heart. She wanted to turn around, to face Dean like he'd done to her earlier, but she couldn't.

She wasn't brave like Tiffany and Jonathan. There was too much at stake for her to act on the feelings that were growing inside of her.

She wanted to love Dean. No, she needed to love Dean. Every part of her was calling out to hold him. To feel his arms around her again. To kiss him like she'd never done before.

But she couldn't.

And she was grateful that she had Penelope in her arms to keep her from doing something completely irrational.

Thankfully, Sondra was close by to shoo them up onto the stage. Just as Jenna started to climb the stairs, Dean's hands rested on her back and arm.

"Let me help," he whispered.

Jenna's whole body responded to the feeling of his hands on

her body and the warmth of his breath on her cheek. She wanted to fall hard and fast into the feelings that were coursing through her.

She was finding it impossible to pull away. To convince herself that she couldn't be with him. That she should tell him no and walk away for good.

They made their way to the stage, and Dean led Jenna over to the manger. Jenna noticed that Dean kept his hand on her back as he guided her. Then he stood next to her as she laid Penelope into the manger and crouched down next to it.

Jimmy was talking in the background, but she couldn't really focus on what he was saying. Instead, she stared at Penelope, fearing what she might do if she looked up at Dean.

And all she wanted to do was look at him.

He sat down on a stool but remained close to her. As if letting her go was the last thing he wanted.

"Jenna," he whispered as he leaned closer.

Jenna allowed the warmth of being near Dean to wash through her body. She closed her eyes for a moment, memorizing how this felt. All her life, she'd never felt as complete as she did right then.

"Please," she whispered, choking back the fear that surfaced inside of her. It was a polarizing feeling, her heart wanting him to stay, her head saying he needed to leave.

"Jenna, I have to tell you," Dean tried again.

Jenna opened her eyes as her brothers gathered around them. Jimmy was talking about the wise men, and Jenna was trying to focus.

"Don't," she whispered as tears began to form on her eyelids.

She felt Dean tense up next to her as her single word settled around them. Then she felt him straighten.

"I know you're scared. I'm scared. But I have to tell you."

"What are you doing, man?" Jackson whispered.

If Dean cared how her brothers felt about what he was

doing, it didn't stop him. "Jenna, I love you. I loved you for a long time before I realized how I felt." From the corner of her eye, Jenna saw Dean shake his head as if he were cursing himself.

It was adorable that he was so tongue-tied. Jenna wanted him to continue but knew he needed to stop. He was going down a path that he couldn't come back from.

"Dude, what?" Josh asked, turning to face Dean.

Jimmy was still reading, but Jenna could feel her dad and her mom staring at them. People in the audience were also looking a little shocked that everyone seemed to be breaking from character.

"Why would you say that to Jenna?" Jackson asked, turning to face Dean.

Unable to hold in the sob, Jenna's tears flowed down her face. "Dean, don't. Please."

"Yeah, what are you doing?" Josh asked.

Jimmy had stopped reading. Sondra had joined them on the stage, and Beth had straightened in the chair she was sitting on. She had a look of pain on her face as she leaned forward. Probably hoping to catch whatever they were saying on stage.

"Are you hitting on my sister?" Jackson asked. He looked angry and hurt as he moved closer to Dean.

"I'm not hitting on her. I love her," Dean said as he studied Jackson and then dropped his gaze to Jenna. The look of desperation in his gaze caused Jenna's heart to hurt.

"And I told you we can't be together," Jenna said, her voice barely above a whisper.

"Be together? Has something been happening?" Josh asked. It wasn't until all of her brothers were standing around her that Jenna realized how formidable they looked.

Desperate to calm them down, Jenna stood and raised her hands. "Dean and I kissed at Jonathan's wedding. He's not just coming on to me."

"You what?" Jonathan asked.

Jenna winced as she shook her head. "Guys, this is Dean we're talking about here." Jenna had known her brothers wouldn't be too happy when they found out, but this felt like an overreaction.

Penelope started to wail, and everyone's attention dropped to the baby in the manger. Layla pushed through the group and reached down to grab her.

"Enough of this," Sondra hissed as she glanced out to the audience and gave them a smile. "We're here to give these people a Christmas to remember. So finish up, and we'll discuss this at home."

Jenna and the three Braxton boys nodded. Dean looked broken as he sighed and nodded as well.

Jimmy finished reading the story, and there was sparse applause as Jenna stood to take a bow. But as she did, she saw Dean pull his head cover off and leave the stage, disappearing into the kitchen.

Jenna thought about going after him but then stopped herself. She doubted that he wanted to talk to her. And she didn't want to hurt him any more than she already had.

When she finally stepped off the stage, she felt a hand on her arm. Sondra pulled her to the side with a disgruntled expression on her face.

"Ma," Jenna said as she pulled her arm away.

Sondra turned her around to face her. "What was that?" she asked as she folded her arms.

Not wanting to go ten rounds with her mom, Jenna sighed. "What was what?"

Sondra narrowed her eyes. "Don't sass me. What was that with Dean?"

Jenna felt tears prick her eyes once more. She was still trying to deal with what Dean had said, and her mom's accusatory stare wasn't helping. Jenna's emotions were out of whack, and she didn't need Sondra jumping to conclusions.

"Mom, please leave it alone," Jenna said, a wave of exhaustion rushing over her as she turned away.

"Leave it alone? Jenna, this is Dean we're talking about. Not some guy you decided to bring home and then dump two days later."

Anger. Frustration. Rage. They all coursed through Jenna as she whipped around. "Well, if I didn't feel like I was this huge disappointment to you by coming home single, maybe I wouldn't have brought so many guys home."

Her words came out louder and sharper than she'd anticipated. But they rang true. "You put so much pressure on your kids to get married, to have babies, that everyone is scared to talk to you."

Jenna was yelling now. And she knew she shouldn't take her failures out on her mom, but she was in pain and finding it hard to stop.

"Jenna, come on, let's go home."

A yell drew everyone's attention over to the nearest table. Beth was propping herself up with one hand and Jordan was letting out an "Eww!" and pointing to the puddle of water on the ground.

Everything that had upset Jenna flew from her mind. She could deal with her broken love life another day. All the Braxtons flew into action as they began to gather up their belongings.

Josh had abandoned all his stuff at the table and was focused on guiding Beth from the room. Thankfully, everyone seemed to know what was going on and quickly moved out of the way.

Sondra was shouting orders to those who were left. They shuffled out of the dining room, leaving Jenna alone. She couldn't help but glance over toward the kitchen. Dean had left that way.

She wondered if he was in his office. He wouldn't have heard the commotion if he was back there.

And she knew he would kick himself for not being there for Josh's new baby. So she swallowed down the fear that crept up inside of her and made her way into the kitchen.

She'd been right; Dean's door was closed. Jenna stood outside of it with her hand raised, ready to knock.

"Can I help you with something?" Nancy asked, appearing next to her.

Jenna stepped back, dropping her hand at the same time. She studied Nancy and nodded. "Beth's water broke. I wanted to tell Dean."

Nancy reached out and rested her hand on Jenna's shoulders. "I've learned that when Dean has that look of pain in his eyes, it's best to leave him alone." She gently guided Jenna back toward the dining room. "I'll let him know. You go be with your brother."

Jenna parted her lips, but before she could say anything, she found herself gently shoved out of the kitchen. Realizing she wasn't getting past Dean's bodyguard, Jenna tightened her jacket and ducked her head.

Nancy was probably right. It was best if she left Dean alone for a bit. Even though it broke her heart, she shouldn't force herself onto him.

There was no way they could still be friends. That ship had sailed. Silently slipping from Dean's life seemed like the most charitable thing she could do. And even though it was breaking her heart, she was going to do it.

No matter how hard it was for her to hear, or how painful it would be for her to say it, she knew in her heart what she felt.

She loved Dean Diego. With every fiber of her being, she loved him.

She just couldn't have him.

DEAN

In his office, Dean paced with his hands on the back of his neck. He stared at the floor and cursed himself for being so stupid.

Why had he professed his love for Jenna during the Nativity scene, right in front of her brothers? What had started out as an act of bravery had quickly turned into an act of stupidity.

"Idiot," he muttered under his breath as he stopped pacing and just stood there, staring at his shoes.

There was no way he'd be able to take that back. Everyone had heard. Josh, Jonathan, and Jackson hadn't looked too pleased with him as they stared him down. And Jenna's tears?

That was what had him the most worried. The last thing any guy wants to have happen when they profess their love is for the girl to burst into tears.

A soft knock on the door drew his attention. Dean dropped his hands and cleared his throat. He'd abandoned his Joseph outfit for a pair of jeans and a sweatshirt that he'd tucked into the corner of his office for emergencies.

"Come in," he said. He winced as he realized it might be a

Braxton, or worse, Sondra, coming in to ask him who the heck he thought he was.

But there was nothing he could do to stop it now. The door slid open, and when Dean saw Nancy, his shoulders relaxed and he blew out his breath. She offered him a sympathetic smile as she slipped into his office, shutting the door behind her.

"The Braxtons have left," she said as she made her way over to the armchair across from his desk and sat down. She rested her elbows on the armrests and steepled her fingers in front of her.

Dean tried to absorb some of her relaxed energy and sat down behind his desk. He adjusted his seat a few times, but nothing seemed right. He was anxious and annoyed with himself for confessing his love to Jenna. He was an idiot. End of story.

"What happened?" Nancy asked, her eyebrows raised.

Dean leaned forward and took a drink of his now cold coffee. It tasted disgusting, but he needed something to help bolster his spirits if he was going to lay his feelings for Jenna out in the open.

"I'm in love with Jenna," he said after he set his mug down. He stared at his desk, unable to look up. He'd already faced so much disappointment with the Braxton family, he couldn't imagine how Nancy would feel. Was the idea of him and Jenna that awful?

"And?" Nancy asked a few seconds later.

Confused, Dean glanced up to see Nancy's earnest expression. It was almost as if she'd known all along.

Dean leaned forward and pressed his hand to his desk. "I'm in love with Jenna Braxton. You know, the family that took me in?"

Nancy nodded with each statement. "I'm aware of the Braxtons, and I'm aware of your situation with them." Nancy furrowed her brow as she touched her forefinger to her lip. "What I don't understand is why you think this is a bad thing."

Dean collapsed back into his chair. "You weren't out there. You didn't hear their reaction." Dean closed his eyes. His heart felt as if there were a vice around it, squeezing and squeezing and not letting go.

Nancy snorted. Confused by her reaction, Dean glanced up to see Nancy covering her mouth as she laughed.

"What?" he asked, feeling a little taken aback by her reaction.

Nancy shook her head for moment before she cleared her throat and straightened. "Did any of them have even an inkling that you cared about Jenna? That Jenna cares about you?"

Dean shrugged. "No. But that...Jenna cares about me?" Why would Nancy say that?

Nancy sighed. "I saw you two dancing. That woman obviously loves you. It's written all over her face."

Dean parted his lips, but nothing came out. He sat there, stunned, staring at Nancy.

He'd assumed that Jenna loved him. And he knew he felt things when he held her, when she looked up at him. But she was constantly denying she felt anything for him. And then she'd brought a guy home for the holidays.

But having someone else confirm what he'd thought all along? He wasn't sure what to do with that. Or what to say.

Nancy was studying him when he looked up at her. She had a smile playing on her lips as she raised her eyebrows. "So, what are you going to do?"

Dean couldn't seem to figure that out either. What *was* he going to do? Everything he'd thought he should do—take charge and confess his love to Jenna—had been a gigantic fail.

Dean rubbed his temples as he rested his elbows on the desk in front of him. "What am I supposed to do?"

"I think you know."

Dean studied Nancy. "I really don't."

"What's the one thing keeping you from Jenna? Besides her inability to admit how she feels about you?" Nancy leaned forward, and Dean could see the anticipation on her face.

He blew out his breath as he shrugged. "Fear that I'm going to lose the only family I really have."

Nancy scoffed

"Besides you," he added.

She nodded. "Well, what if the Braxton family accepted your feelings? What then?"

Dean narrowed his eyes as he tried to piece together what she was saying. "So if I get everyone to sign off on my love for Jenna, then we can be together?" He bounced back onto his chair. "Doesn't that seem a little childish?"

Why should he have to ask his family to accept his feelings for Jenna?

"If your main worry is that you'll lose your family, then that's a step you'll have to take. I'm sure once they see how serious you are about her, they won't stop you." Nancy smiled at him. "They love you, and they love Jenna."

Dean nodded. What Nancy was saying was starting to make sense.

"And if Jenna sees how her family feels, maybe she'll be more willing to take the leap."

Dean was starting to like this plan.

"And if not, at least you won't have to hold onto this secret anymore. You can all move on and finally start to heal." Nancy leaned back and brushed her hands together as if she'd just finished a job well done.

Dean mulled over what she'd said and then sighed. He was still worried about what might happen, but he had faith that the Braxtons cared about him. And Nancy had hit the nail on the head. He'd hated holding onto this secret about him and Jenna.

He hated how he couldn't talk to Jackson about it for fear that he would lose his friend. Putting everything into the open was just what he needed to either win Jenna back or move on.

Nancy sighed as she rubbed her hands on her thighs and stood. She nodded to Dean and slipped back out to the kitchen.

Now alone, Dean tipped his head back and blew out his breath. He knew what he needed to do, and he was going to do it. No matter how much coming clean scared him, he had to have faith that the Braxtons would still love him—still look at him as family—regardless of his feelings for Jenna.

And maybe, just maybe, if Jenna saw that her family was okay with his feelings for her, that might just give Jenna the confidence to love him back.

There was a quick knock on Dean's door, and Nancy looked sheepish as she stuck her head back into the room.

"I forgot to tell you. Beth went into labor. Everyone is at the hospital."

Dean stood so fast his chair flew into the wall behind him. He grabbed his jacket. "I'm going," he said as he rushed to the door. He glanced down at Nancy. "Can you handle things here?"

Nancy smiled and patted him on the shoulder. "Of course. I've got your back." She gave him a wink and then shooed him away. "Go."

Dean shot her a thankful smile and strode through the kitchen and out the back door. He pulled his jacket closer around his body as he climbed into his car and started the engine. Then he put the car into reverse and focused on driving to the hospital.

He pushed aside all his fears as he drove, his knuckles turning white. This was his family, and no matter what happened between him and Jenna, he wasn't going to go anywhere.

He was a Braxton through and through.

After parking, he made his way into the hospital and up to the maternity ward. The elevator dinged and the doors slid open. Just as he walked out, Jackson exited a room to his left with a cup of coffee in his hand.

Their gazes met, and Jackson's eyebrows rose. They stood there for a moment, and Dean had a sudden urge to apologize. He'd broken the best friend and brother code. He should have known better.

"Listen..." Dean started, and then his eyes widened as Jackson walked up to him.

Jackson paused for a second and pulled Dean into a hug. "Sorry for freaking out earlier," he said as he pulled back.

Dean wasn't sure what was going on. He returned the hug and then glanced up at his friend. Was he serious, or was this a joke? But Jackson looked completely calm as he sipped his coffee.

Dean cleared his throat. "I should be the one apologizing. I shouldn't have lied to you."

Jackson furrowed his brow. "When did you lie to me?" Then recognition dawned as he nodded. "The girl you were talking about when I was at your house. That was Jenna?"

Dean ran his hands through his hair and nodded. "Yeah."

Jackson studied him for a moment and then shrugged. "Listen, if you want to take on Jenna, then you have my blessing." He smiled.

"Really?"

Jackson nodded and sipped his coffee. "Hey, if Jenna was going to be with anyone, it might as well be you. I know you wouldn't break her heart. You'd be too scared." Jackson reached out and punched Dean in the shoulder.

"Oh really?" Dean asked.

Isabel came out of the same door as Jackson with a water bottle in hand. She paused. "What are you two doing?" she asked as she walked up to them.

Jackson stepped back and pointed at Dean. "Dean was challenging me to a duel."

Isabel rolled her eyes as she slipped her arm through Jackson's. "You two. Will it ever end?"

Jackson chuckled as he leaned over and kissed her on top of her head. "Probably not."

Dean focused on Isabel. "How are you feeling?" he asked. He cared about his sister-in-law. It broke his heart that she was hurting.

Isabel's expression softened for a moment before she gave him a smile. "It's still hard, but we're making our way through it." She rested her head on Jackson's shoulder.

"If you need anything, I'm here." Dean wasn't sure what he could do to help, he just wanted her to know he cared.

Isabel gave him a small smile. "Thanks for talking to this guy over here; it helped."

Dean nodded. "Well, it was pretty easy. You guys have a great marriage, and he was being a dork." He winked at Isabel as Jackson's jaw dropped.

They started walking down the hallway. Dean hesitated, worrying about what he would find when he got around the rest of the family. Jackson must have sensed his hesitation because he turned around and smiled.

"Come on. No one hates you. I'm pretty sure Jonathan has moved on, and Josh is with Beth. I'm pretty sure thoughts about you and Jenna haven't even crossed his mind."

Dean studied Jackson for a moment and then nodded. He was right. Dean was being selfish worrying about himself. He was here for Josh and Beth. That should be his focus.

Jackson and Isabel led him into the waiting room. TVs lined the walls, and it took Dean a second to find Jenna. She was still in her Mary costume and was sitting with her feet tucked under her and her arm resting on the back of the bench. Her head was resting on her arm as she watched one of the TVs.

"Dean," Sondra said as she stood and made her way over to him. She didn't hesitate to wrap her arms around him and pull him close. "I'm so happy you came," she said, leaning back to smile at him.

Warmth spread through Dean as he smiled down at Sondra. From the corner of his eye, he saw Jenna tense, but she didn't look at him.

"I'm sorry. I should have come sooner," he said.

Sondra shushed him. "Nonsense. We shouldn't have overreacted." She reached up and patted his cheek. "Jenna told us everything. We're just happy you forgave us for jumping to conclusions."

Dean shrugged, wondering for a moment what Jenna had said. Did he dare hope it was positive?

"That's what family is for, right? Always being there for each other, even when you fight."

Sondra nodded, her eyes filling with tears. "Yes. Always." Her gaze slipped over to Isabel and Jackson, who were sitting next to each other. They were talking, but they must have sensed Sondra's gaze because a moment later they glanced up.

It was almost as if Sondra had sensed something was off between them all along.

"Thanks," Dean said. He was ready to collapse on the nearest chair and take a deep breath.

Sondra nodded and then hurried over to Jackson and Isabel and sat next to them. A few minutes later, Sondra sobbed as she pulled Isabel into her arms.

Everyone glanced over, but Sondra didn't seem to mind. She had both Jackson and Isabel wrapped in her arms. A sense of relief washed over Dean as he realized how freeing the truth was.

Jackson and Isabel looked sad but happy that they'd finally told Sondra. They looked like Dean felt. Happy that the truth was out there but sad with the situation in general.

Dean couldn't help himself as his gaze slipped to Jenna. Her head was still down, and she was drawing circles on the chair.

She looked so small. So fragile. And all Dean wanted to do was pull her into his arms and hold her. Protect her like she deserved.

Dean stood and began to walk over to Jenna. He hoped it looked like he wanted a magazine from the coffee table in front of her, instead of wanting to talk to her.

Just as he bent down to pick up a magazine, Sondra's voice startled him.

"I'm glad you two are together," she said, standing next to him and pointedly looking at him and Jenna. "I was hoping I could depend on you to go back and get Christmas dinner warming. Everything's made-up, it just needs to go into the oven." Sondra smiled at them in that mischievous way she did when she had ulterior motives.

"Mom," Jenna said. She cast an annoyed glace in Sondra's direction.

Dean couldn't help but study her. Jenna looked tired as she pushed her hair from her face. But she also never looked more beautiful. He couldn't deny the feelings that were coursing through him.

And for the first time, he allowed them.

"It's okay. I can go by myself if Jenna wants to stay," he said.

Jenna studied him and then sighed. "It's fine. We can go together." She gave Sondra one more glance before standing. Then she grabbed her jacket and wandered out of the waiting room and over to the elevator.

Dean watched her go and then glanced down at Sondra, who was staring up at him. She wiggled her eyebrows as she bumped Dean with her hip.

"Go get her," she said and then began pushing him toward the elevator.

"Go what?" Dean asked, trying to process what she'd said.

"Jenna. Go get her."

Dean swallowed as he allowed Sondra to push him out of the

waiting room. The elevator buzzed as Jenna held the door open for him.

He boarded the elevator, and Jenna pressed the door close button.

Now alone, Dean glanced over at Jenna, who was standing in the corner with her arms folded. She was staring a little too hard at the floor in front of her.

The elevator descended and opened. The car was deafeningly silent as Dean tried not to stare at Jenna. He didn't want to creep her out, but he needed to know what she was feeling.

But she was like a steel trap. He couldn't tell how she felt at all.

And it was driving him crazy.

He followed her through the hospital doors and out to the parking lot. Jenna slowed and glanced over at him as if she were expecting him to lead the way.

"Come on," he said as he led her over to his car and pulled out his keys.

Jenna nodded as she pulled open the passenger door and slipped onto the seat. Dean took a moment to gather his thoughts and climbed into the driver's seat. He started the engine and pulled out of the parking spot.

By the end of the day, Dean was going to tell her exactly how he felt. He wasn't worried about anything anymore. All he knew was that not being with Jenna was a whole lot scarier than being with her. He was willing to take that chance now.

After all, what did he have to lose?

JENNA

J enna focused on the road as Dean drove through Honey Grove. She'd wrapped her arms around her chest and was attempting to calm her racing thoughts.

She wasn't sure what was happening. In the waiting room of the hospital, she'd tried to convince herself that what Dean had been trying to tell her during the Nativity play didn't mean anything. That her heart didn't pound when Dean was around. That she didn't care what he was trying to say.

But by the time Dean pulled up next to her parents' house, Jenna was pretty sure her heart was going to burst from her chest. Her conversation with her family had been short. She'd explained what happened at Jonathan's wedding. How she'd broken things off, and how she'd tried to forget him.

Thankfully, the shock of her relationship with Dean seemed to have worn off. Instead of being angry with her, her brothers had just stared at her like she had two heads.

They were trying to figure out why she felt she needed to hide her relationship. If she cared for Dean and he cared for her, why weren't they seeing each other?

Jenna didn't know why, but hearing that from her family had

helped her. She'd been so wrapped up in doing what she thought her family wanted her to do—in trying to live up to her mother's expectations—that her own desires had been crushed.

Once she heard Dean mumble out his feelings for her, she realized she didn't care what anybody else thought. Her family could complain about who she dated all they wanted to, but it didn't mean she was going to listen.

If she wanted to be single, great. If she wanted to love Dean, she was going to do that. She was no longer going to live in fear. She would be honest and open with them about what was going on, and then she would leave it at that.

Having her family get on board with her new relationship felt weird. But also freeing. She didn't need her family's blessing, but it was nice to have.

And then when Dean walked into the waiting room, she felt as if she would melt right there. Especially when she felt his gaze on her. Or when he stared down at her like she was the only one that mattered.

As much as it annoyed her that Sondra had shoved them together, she was ready to lay everything on the line. To tell Dean exactly what she wanted him to know.

She loved him.

"We're here," Dean said softly as he pulled the keys from the ignition and slipped them into his jacket pocket.

Jenna nodded and pulled on the door handle and got out. She paused, waiting for Dean to round the car. His eyebrows rose as she fell into step with him.

She could fell that he was tense. It was emanating from him. She wanted to calm him down, but she wanted to get inside before the in-depth conversation started.

Thankfully, her mother had given all of them a key to the house. Jenna unlocked the front door, and she and Dean walked in. The house smelled like mulled cider and pumpkin pie.

Jenna took a deep breath and closed her eyes for a

moment, a sense of completeness washing over her. This was where she wanted to be. Right here with her family at Christmas. And with Dean, who she hoped and prayed would forgive her.

"Let me," Dean offered, reaching out to help her slip off her jacket.

Jenna's cheeks flushed as she nodded and turned so her back was to him. His fingers grazed her shoulders, and even though she was wearing a couple layers of fabric, it didn't matter. Her body knew what it was like to be touched by him. And it longed for it.

But confessing her love in this Mary getup wasn't on her list of romantic fantasies, so she turned and gave him a sheepish smile.

"I'm going to go change quick. I'll be back in a second. Mom said all the food is in the fridge. We just need to turn the oven on."

Dean's gaze slipped over to the kitchen, and he nodded. "Got it. I can do that."

Jenna started up the stairs and then stopped, realizing there was no way she could undo the zipper on her dress. Her entire body warmed at the thought of what she was going to ask him.

Clearing her throat, she decided to charge ahead. "Do you mind?" she asked as she pulled her hair away from her neck and waved toward the zipper. "I don't think I can reach it."

Dean's eyes widened as his gaze slipped to her shoulders and then down her back. He swallowed and nodded as he stepped closer to her.

Her skin tingled as he gripped the top of her dress with one hand. Then the pressure around her chest lessened as he slid the zipper down to her lower back, right above her underwear.

"There," he said, his voice gruff and low.

Jenna's stomach did a somersault as she glanced over her shoulder at him. His gaze met hers, and there was a need there.

One she'd never seen before, but one she recognized. It was the same need that burned inside of her.

"Dean," she whispered, as she turned around only to have him take a step back.

"Jenna, there's so much I want to say to you, but not like this." He shoved his hands into the front pockets of his jeans. "You need to be dressed before we can talk."

Jenna chewed her lip and then nodded. He was right. So she shot him a quick smile and bolted up the stairs. Her hands were shaking as she slipped out of the dress and into a pair of jeans and a soft green sweater. She took a quick look in the mirror, adjusted her hair, and brushed her teeth.

Once she was confident that she looked presentable, she made her way down the stairs. Butterflies were racing around in her stomach like Jordan after Halloween.

She knew what she wanted. She wanted Dean. She just didn't know how to say it. Or how to apologize for being scared. For running from the one person she was destined to be with.

When she stepped off the last stair, she found Dean leaning on the counter in the kitchen. He was reading something, his hair falling over his forehead just so. Jenna's hands itched to feel the soft strands of his hair. To run her fingers through it.

She wanted to touch him. No, she needed to touch him. Like she needed to breathe.

Her only hope was that he felt the same way too.

Dean must have heard her come in, because he straightened and his gaze fell on her. A look passed over his face, and it took her breath away. She'd never felt this way before. She loved the appreciation that a man could give in just a look.

She wanted more of it. She wanted all of Dean.

"You look beautiful," he said. His voice was low and full of emotion. It sent tingles up and down her spine.

Her cheeks heated as she stepped closer to him. "Thanks,"

she whispered as she tucked her hair behind her ear. "You don't look so bad yourself." She was standing a foot away from him now.

She could smell his cologne and feel his warmth next to her. There was something so familiar about being next to him. It was like she'd finally come home. This was where she belonged. She'd fought it for so long, but now that she was here, she knew she could never leave.

Dean was hers, forever.

So, she threw caution to the wind and reached up to push his hair from his forehead. Dean's eyes widened as he met her gaze. There was a desire there. She could see he felt the same.

"Jenna, I—"

"I love you, Dean," she said as she inched closer to him. He'd been so honest and forthright with her—it was her turn to do the same.

He deserved better than her, yes. But no one would love him like she would.

When he didn't answer right away, Jenna glanced up to see him staring at her. She blinked a few times, wondering if she'd said the wrong thing.

"Dean?" she asked. Had she misread the entire situation? Was everything that he'd said at the Nativity a joke?

Suddenly, his hand was around her waist, and he was pulling her toward him, closing the gap between their bodies. He cradled her head in his hand and stared into her eyes.

"Did you just say you love me?" he asked. His voice was soft and low. Like he was worried the question would scare her away.

Wanting to prove to him that she meant it, Jenna rose up onto her toes and pressed her lips to his. Dean kissed her back, softly and gently.

Jenna pulled back and nodded. "Yes, I love you," she said slowly, letting each word roll off her tongue.

Dean's eyes glistened as he stared at her. "I love you," he whispered, tipping his forehead down and resting it on hers.

Jenna laughed as she smiled up at him. "Good. 'Cause I'm not going anywhere this time. I'm here to stay."

Dean pulled back and studied her. Then he leaned down and crushed his lips to hers.

And Jenna kissed him. With all the passion and love that she'd been denying. She wanted him to know, really know, with every fiber of his being, that she was his. For good.

Dean wrapped his arms around her and lifted her up. He carried her over to the counter and set her on it. Jenna wrapped her legs around his waist as she deepened the kiss.

They fell into this dance. This discovery. Kissing as if this was the first time. And maybe it was. There was no fear this time. No worry of disappointing their family or each other.

Now, she could just be a woman loving a man. They weren't anything other than Jenna and Dean.

Jenna wasn't sure how long the kiss lasted. If it went on forever, she would be completely content.

But, when Dean pulled back and rested the palms of his hands against her cheeks, Jenna laughed.

Dean studied her. "Say it again."

"What?"

Dean met her gaze, the need inside it deepening. "Tell me you love me. I'm scared I didn't hear it."

Jenna reached out and rested her hand on his forearm. She pinched her lips together for a moment and then said, "I love you, Dean. You are my person. You are the one I want to love forever."

Dean studied her and leaned forward to press his lips to hers once more. When he pulled back, Jenna groaned. This was the least fun game.

Dean chuckled. "Hang on, I want to say something," Dean said as Jenna tried to pull him back to her.

She blew out her breath. "Okay."

He smiled. "I love you. And it's about time you figured out that you're my person."

Jenna scoffed as she swatted at his shoulder. "Hey!" she protested.

Dean chuckled and then wrapped his arm around her waist. "This is going to be fun."

———

Two hours later, Jenna got a call from Sondra. Beth gave birth to a healthy, albeit loud, baby girl. Jenna cheered, and Dean shot her a confused expression as he basted the ham that he'd put in the oven to warm.

Jenna pointed to her stomach and tried to imitate a person giving birth, which was lost on Dean. He just stared at her like she was a crazy person.

"Beth had the baby," Jenna squealed.

Dean shot a thumbs-up in her direction.

"Dean said congrats," Jenna said.

Sondra paused. "Does this mean…?"

Jenna felt the permanent smile on her lips deepen. As rocky as her relationship was with her mom, she couldn't imagine telling her news to anyone else. Sure, Sondra was annoyingly obsessed with getting her kids married, but she had a good heart.

And, annoyingly, she always knew exactly what her kids needed.

"Let's just say feelings were shared, and now we're seeing how it fits."

Sondra cheered so loud that Jenna had to hold the phone away from her ear. "It's a Christmas miracle!" could be heard on the other end.

Dean furrowed his brow as he slid the ham back into the

oven and shut the door. Then realization dawned, and he chuckled as he folded his arms and leaned against the counter.

"I'll see you guys when you get back," she said as she hung up the phone, doubting her mother was even listening anymore.

Just as she set her phone on the counter, Dean appeared and wrapped both arms around her, planting a kiss on her forehead. He chuckled, causing Jenna to glance up at him.

"What?"

He shrugged. "I'm just glad I get to kiss you anytime I want to now." He pressed his lips to the tip of her nose.

Jenna laughed as she rested her hands on his chest, reveling in the feeling of his heartbeat against her fingertips. "Well, as long as you always do what I ask and never question me, I'm here for the kissing."

Dean pulled back. "Ooh, a challenge." He pulled her closer. "I'm game."

Jenna snuggled into his chest and sighed. "Promise me you'll never leave?"

"Promise me you'll always love me?"

Jenna peeked up at him. "Deal."

Dean leaned in. "Deal," he whispered as he pressed his lips to hers.

Jenna couldn't help but feel completely and utterly at peace, standing in her parents' kitchen and kissing Dean. This was where she was meant to be. This was the man she was meant to love.

She was complete.

Once and for all, she was home. And she was never leaving again.

EPILOGUE

Dean

Dean leaned against the kitchen counter later that night, watching Sondra and Jenna talk. They were standing in front of the sink. Sondra's arms were elbow deep in the sudsy water while Jenna stood next to her with a towel in hand.

They were talking and laughing. Dean wasn't listening to what they were saying, he was just enjoying the fact that, for once in his life, he felt complete. This was his home. He loved Jenna. He couldn't imagine his life going any more perfectly.

Christmas dinner had been amazing—and it wasn't just because he had a great companion next to him. He and Jenna had worked hard to get the table set and the food ready for when the Braxtons returned.

As soon as they came bursting in through the door, dinner was in full swing. Nancy and Naomi showed up and had a good time. Thankfully, Naomi had noticed the change in Dean and Jenna and remained platonic for the evening. She smiled and ate and then excused herself once dinner wound down.

Nancy was camped out on the couch with Jordan, reading books and eating Sondra's famous cookies. Josh had stayed at the hospital with Beth, and Sondra had sent Jimmy back with a cooler full of Christmas dinner.

Jackson and Isabel were curled up in the back room with Tiffany and Jonathan, watching a Hallmark Christmas movie. James and Layla were in the living room with Nancy and Jordan, playing with Penelope.

Everything in the house seemed at peace. Everyone was happy. Dean never thought he could feel this way before, and he never wanted it to end.

He never wanted to take for granted what he had here with the Braxtons. He'd been so close to walking away, and he would have always regretted that.

As his gaze landed on Jenna, he knew what he wanted. He wanted her. Forever.

He wanted to marry that woman. To take her into his arms and never let her go. He wanted to raise kids with her. Kids that would only know the love of a family, not the pain of loss.

And he wanted to start that journey right now.

Dean excused himself from the kitchen and headed over to Jackson, who looked like he was about to fall asleep. Isabel poked him a few times, reminding him he'd promised to stay awake.

As soon as Dean walked into the room, Jonathan and Jackson perked up.

"Hey, man," Jackson said with his eyes wide. He looked desperate to be anywhere but where he was.

"Yeah, what's up?" Jonathan asked.

Dean chuckled. "I was wondering if you guys could help me with something."

Jonathan and Jackson were on their feet in an instant. They crossed the room and clapped him on the shoulder.

"We're here for you, man," Jackson said.

Isabel snorted and Jackson turned to shrug at her. "Dean needs my help."

Isabel shot him a look and then reached out to grab a bowl of chocolates. She handed Tiffany one. "Our men are abandoning us. How rude."

Tiffany nodded as she took the chocolate. "So rude."

Dean cast an apologetic smile their way, but he doubted they saw it as Jonathan and Jackson dragged him from the room.

"So what's up? What do you need our help with?" Jonathan asked.

Dean pressed his finger to his lips as they slipped up the stairs. Jenna and Sondra were still in the kitchen, and he didn't want them to know what was happening.

Once they were upstairs and behind a closed door, Dean turned to them as he rubbed his hands together. "I have an idea," he said.

His brothers nodded.

"I want to propose to Jenna. Tonight."

Their eyes widened as a small smile spread across their lips. After they glanced at one another, they turned back to Dean.

"Tell us what you want us to do," Jonathan said.

EPILOGUE

Sondra

Sondra collapsed on a chair next to her sister, Priscilla, and let out an exhausted groan. The music on the speakers was blaring as the entire Braxton family, extended and immediate, paraded around on the dance floor.

Jenna was in her white dress, looking as beautiful as ever. Dean was spinning her around, and Sondra couldn't help but feel complete as she stared at her daughter.

This was what she'd always wanted for her kids. For them to find someone to love. To create a life together that was their own. And being here, at her youngest child's wedding was just the cherry on top of a very sweet cake.

"Exhausted?" Priscilla asked as she glanced over at Sondra.

Sondra nodded and reached forward to grab the flute of champagne that a waiter had just dropped off. "Yes, but I'm glad Jenna did it this way. So many of my boys eloped or had small weddings, I'm happy Jenna agreed to a big wedding." Sondra sat back as she smiled.

"You're lucky. I can't seem to get any of my children to

marry. They're all work and no play." Priscilla said as she waved at her two sons and three daughters that were scattered around the room.

Sondra glanced over at Priscilla with a sympathetic expression. She knew what that was like. Wishing and hoping for new family members and grandkids. She didn't envy her younger sister.

"Eh, it'll happen. I swear I had that same thought just a year ago, and now, all my kids are married and having babies of their own."

Josh and Beth were on the dance floor. Jordan was next to them with baby Jojo in his arms. He was twirling her around, and from what Sondra could see, Josh was telling him to slow down.

Sondra had sensed that Jordan hadn't been too happy with the idea of getting a baby sister. But now that Jojo was here, he was the most overprotective brother she'd ever seen. It took a semitruck to separate the two.

"I keep telling myself that, but it doesn't seem to make a difference." Priscilla downed her champagne and flagged down a waiter for another.

Sondra reached out and patted her sister's hand. "I know. You just have to have faith." Then she allowed a mischievous smile to spread across her lips. "Or we could do a little meddling. All my kids are married now. Maybe it's time we start working on yours."

Priscilla glanced over at her. "Really?"

Sondra shrugged. "What could it hurt?"

Jonathan and Tiffany stood up, and Sondra glanced over to watch Tiffany waddle onto the dance floor with Jonathan behind her. They just found out that they were having twin boys and Sondra couldn't be happier. The more babies to hold, the better.

Priscilla tapped her fingers on the table. "Do you think you'll have time? I mean with Isabel and Jackson waiting to hear from the adoption agency, I don't want you to not be there for them."

After losing the baby before Christmas, Jackson and Isabel decided that they wanted to try adoption. They were hoping to adopt a little girl from Korea and were just waiting to hear back.

Sondra shrugged. "I'm super woman. I can do everything. Besides, with Jimmy retiring and turning the construction company over to James and Josh, he'll be around to help." Sondra leaned in. "And you know how much he loves to meddle in people's lives."

Priscilla snorted. "He'd be better than Bert. He keeps telling me to 'leave the blasted children alone.' " Priscilla pouted as she fiddled with her fork.

"Sondra?" Layla's voice was quiet, and Sondra looked up. Layla was holding a drooling Penelope in her arms. "Mind watching Penelope for us? We wanted to dance."

James was standing behind Layla with what looked like desperation in his eyes. Penelope's blonde curls bounced as she kicked her legs. Sondra could never pass up the opportunity to hold her grandbaby, so she smiled and held out her arms.

"Of course," she said. Penelope squealed as she wiggled around in Sondra's arms. "I know I've said this already, but you really did an amazing job on Jenna's dress. She looks like an angel."

Layla's cheeks blushed as she nodded and then leaned forward to kiss Sondra on the cheek. "Thanks," she said. James grabbed Layla's hand, and they disappeared onto the dance floor.

Priscilla was cooing at Penelope when Sondra turned her attention back to her sister. There was a look—a very familiar look—in Priscilla's gaze. One that said she was ready. Ready for her kids to marry and give her grandbabies.

The desire to help her sister grew inside of Sondra, so she leaned forward. "Come on, we should try. After all, what harm could happen? Your kids fall in love and give you these?" she asked as she squeezed Penelope and nibbled at her cheek.

Priscilla studied Sondra for a minute and then sighed. "All right, let's do it. And you're right, the worst that could happen is that my kids think I meddle too much, which they already do. But, if we're successful, and my kids finally find love. Well, I'd say it's worth a shot."

Sondra nodded as a resolute feeling rose up inside of her. She was so completely and utterly happy that it hurt. Her family was right where she wanted them to be, with only happiness on the horizon.

And now she wanted it for her baby sister. And she'd help her get it, no matter what.

***

I hope you enjoyed reading the last installment of the Braxton family!

Jenna and Dean made me smile so much.

If you missed the first book of the series, make sure you grab Coming Home to Honey Grove, Josh and Beth's story, HERE

If you're looking for some more Christmas romance, check out, Second Chance at Christmas Inn.
HERE

Also, feel free to pick up your copy of my BRAND NEW series, The Red Stilettos Book Club Romance. The first book is set to release in April, 2020 titled, The Magnolia Inn.

Join my Newsletter!
Find great deals on my books and other sweet romance!
Get, Fighting Love for the Cowboy FREE
just for signing up!
Grab it HERE!

SHE'S AN IRS AUDITOR DESPERATE TO PROVE HERSELF.
HE'S A COWBOY TRYING TO HOLD ONTO HIS RANCH.
LOVE WAS NOT ON THE AGENDA.

OTHER BOOKS BY ANNE-MARIE MEYER

CLEAN ADULT ROMANCES

<u>Forgetting the Billionaire</u>

Book 1 of the Clean Billionaire Romance series

Second Chance Mistletoe Kisses

Book 1 of Love Tries Again series

Second Chance at Christmas Inn

Book 3 of Love Tries Again Series

Coming Home to Honey Grove

Book 1 of A Braxton Family Romance series

Friendship Blooms in Honey Grove

Book 2 of A Braxton Family Romance series

Escaping to Honey Grove

Book 3 of A Braxton Family Romance series

Forgiveness Found in Honey Grove

Book 4 of A Braxton Family Romance series

Christmas in Honey Grove

Book 5 of A Braxton Family Romance series

Her Second Chance

Book 0 of the Braxton Brothers series

Fighting Love for the Cowboy

Book 1 of A Moose Falls Romance

ABOUT THE AUTHOR

Anne-Marie Meyer lives in MN with her husband, four boys, and baby girl. She loves romantic movies and believes that there is a FRIENDS quote for just about every aspect of life.

Connect with Anne-Marie on these platforms!
anne-mariemeyer.com

Made in the USA
Columbia, SC
06 January 2022